"I'd like to continue working here after my baby comes. Don't worry. I can still provide excellent care for your daughter."

"Good." Ryan ran a hand across the back of his neck and looked at a painting on the far wall. Anywhere but at Kelsey's pregnant body. "You'll let me know if anything changes?"

"I'm past six months. The only thing that's going to change is the size of my belly. Women have babies all the time and still take care of their other children." She blushed. "Not that Mariah is my child. I mean... I didn't mean..."

He brought his gaze back to hers. Those charming freckles had appeared, and he was tempted to touch them. "I know what you meant. Feel free to make a nursery out of the extra room."

"That's so nice of you, Ryan. Thank you."

If she didn't stop looking at him that way he wasn't sure what he might do. She made him feel special, important, powerful—like a man who could move mountains.

Kelsey Mason was a dangerous woman. Dangerously beguiling.

Linda Goodnight, a romantic at heart, believes in the traditional values of family and home. Writing books enables her to share her certainty that, with faith and perseverance, love can last forever and happy endings really are possible.

A native of Oklahoma, Linda lives in the country with her husband, Gene, and Mugsy, an adorably obnoxious rat terrier. She and Gene have a blended family of six grown children. A former elementary-school teacher, she is also a licensed nurse. When time permits, Linda loves to read, watch football and rodeo and indulge in chocolate. She also enjoys taking long, calorie-burning walks in the nearby woods. Readers can write to her at linda@lindagoodnight.com.

In January, don't miss Linda's next novel. Set amongst the rugged Rockies, the story features a woman who must face her biggest fear of all…before she can be claimed as *The Snow-Kissed Bride!*

LINDA GOODNIGHT

The Millionaire's Nanny Arrangement

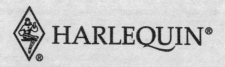

TORONTO • NEW YORK • LONDON
AMSTERDAM • PARIS • SYDNEY • HAMBURG
STOCKHOLM • ATHENS • TOKYO • MILAN • MADRID
PRAGUE • WARSAW • BUDAPEST • AUCKLAND

ISBN-13: 978-0-373-17543-7
ISBN-10:   0-373-17543-4

THE MILLIONAIRE'S NANNY ARRANGEMENT

First North American Publication 2008.

Copyright © 2008 by Linda Goodnight.

www.eHarlequin.com

Printed in U.S.A.

From bump to baby and beyond....

Whether she's expecting or they're adopting—a special arrival is on its way!

Follow the tears and triumphs as these couples find their lives blessed with the magic of parenthood....

In December, escape on a whirlwind to the Amalfi Coast in Italy, where a sexy footballer tries to persuade pregnant Lyssa Belperio that he wants to exchange celebrity bachelorhood for fatherhood!

Pregnant: Father Wanted
Claire Baxter

For all my friends and colleagues at Butner School. Thanks for a million laughs and a lot of great years.

CHAPTER ONE

WITH A JERK, KELSEY MASON opened her eyes and groaned. She squinted at her watch. Nearly twelve hours since her flight had been canceled, stranding her in a strange city, with no money and less hope. The armrest of the standard-issue airport chair jabbed into her back, already achy from the load she carried around her middle. Every bone in her body protested as she rotated forward and straightened.

"You talk in your sleep," a tiny voice commented. "Somb-niloquy."

Swiveling toward the sound, Kelsey was speared by a pair of huge liquid-brown eyes in a face that couldn't be more than six years old.

"You talk pretty big for a little girl." Kelsey stretched, rolling her head on stiff shoulders.

"I'm a genius." The child said it as matter-of-factly as Kelsey would have said, "I'm a teacher." If that was true. Which it wasn't. Not any more anyway. She was no longer a lot of things she'd once been.

Glad for the distraction and amused by the dark-haired angel in front of her, Kelsey shifted around on the miserable chair until she found a comfortable spot for her belly and said, "I've never met a child genius before. What's your name?"

"Pollyanna." A dimple flashed. "Well, not really. I'm reading that book and decided to change my name. My real name is Mariah."

"Pleased to meet you, Mariah. I'm Kelsey." Kelsey smiled in spite of the crick in her neck. "I loved that story, too. Have you seen the movie?"

The child looked shocked. "Absolutely not. Daddy says the book is always better than the movie so you should read before watching and then compare and contrast."

"Daddy is absolutely right." Wherever he was. Kelsey glanced around but spotted no one watching the little girl. The man should be arrested for allowing a child this young to run around a huge airport unsupervised.

"We've been stranded here in Denver all day waiting on clearance. Actually, seventeen hours and twenty-two minutes but that's close enough to a day, don't you think?"

"Yes, I do. I've been here for twelve."

"It's fun, isn't it?" Fun wasn't the exact term Kelsey would use. "There are so many interesting people to talk to. Did you know the man over there," the child pointed, "works for the queen of Netherlands? He's going to send me her autograph. And that lady over there is really upset because her boyfriend moved to Syracuse with his mother. She gave me a dollar to go away. I bought her a cup of coffee with it. Daddy says never take money from strangers."

"Did he ever tell you not to *talk* to strangers?"

"All the time." The child giggled, covering her mouth with both hands. Long dark curls danced around her shoulders. "But I'm discerning."

"What if I were a bad person?"

"Are you?"

"No. I'm a teacher." Or was before she'd given up everything to be Mark's wife. "And I like kids. But I could have been a bad person."

Brown eyes batted in innocence. "What could happen in a crowded airport?"

Well, actually lots of things, but Kelsey wasn't one to frighten small, unattended children. "Bad people have ways."

"But you aren't bad. You're nice. You're having a baby. Mommies are always nice, except I don't have one, but I'm interviewing. Would you like to be interviewed for the position?"

Kelsey laughed, though the sound was hollow and tinged with bitterness. "For the position of mommy?"

"Well, Daddy wants me to have a private tutor-slash-nanny. But I really want a mommy. My first mommy died a long time ago." If the memory pained her, the little girl gave no indication, but Kelsey couldn't stop the sharp pang of sympathy.

"So," the little girl went on, "do you think you could handle both positions?"

For tutor *and* mommy? What an interesting conversation. And Kelsey had no idea how to respond to such a question without treading on unpleasant ground. Fortunately, she didn't have to. At that precise moment, a harried man sprinted toward them. Tie askew, his jacket billowed out at the sides. Kelsey did her best not to notice the lean, lanky, fit body beneath.

"Mariah!"

A radiant smile lit the little girl's face. "There comes my daddy. He's nice. You'll like him."

Considering that she'd already formed a negative opinion of the man, Kelsey doubted it. Especially now that she saw him. Even without her contacts, she would have noticed this guy and run the other way—if she could move that fast. Tall and dark, with hair and eyes that matched his daughter's, he was too good-looking. Too successful-looking, too. And she was so off good-looking, successful men it wasn't even funny.

The child leaned in and whispered conspiratorially, "He's been really depressed lately. Almost clinical. Don't tell him I mentioned it, but I thought you should know. It's the whole thing with that Dallas Businessman of the Year Award and the pressure of success. Being discerning as I am, I can tell. It's such a trial for him to deal with a genius child and run a multi-million dollar operation. So, if I can just find a mommy to keep me under control and out of his hair while he works, I'm sure he'll be better."

Kelsey stared at the child and then at the father, coming toward them like a stealth bomber, fast and furious, sleek and dangerous. It really irked her that this bright child thought she was a bother to her father. How unfair, and what a jerk he must be to make her feel that way.

"Daddy, come on over and meet my friend, Kelsey. She's having a baby, and I'm interviewing her for the job."

The man closed his eyes briefly and shook his head, hands on hips to catch his breath from what must have been a jog around the concourse.

"I apologize for my daughter, Miss—" When she only stared instead of filling in the blank, he finished with "—Kelsey. I'm Ryan Storm."

His name sent a shock wave through her. Ryan Storm? *Ohmigosh.* It couldn't be. But a second look through squinted eyes confirmed it. It *was* him. Ryan Storm, backstreet boy of Bartlett High turned Wall Street wonder, all grown up and looking good. Real good.

He didn't know it, but she'd once had a crush on him, most likely because he'd been so unsuitable for a goody-two-shoes who never broke the rules.

She'd always had lousy taste in men.

"You've already met my errant child, Mariah, who will likely be the death of me." He took the little girl by the hand. Mariah beamed up at him with unabashed adoration. "I'm sorry if she was bothering you."

"She's actually very entertaining." And you should have known where she was.

"That's one word for it."

Mariah at his side, he slid into the chair next to Kelsey, bringing with him the scent of a very recognizable and equally expensive men's cologne. How could he smell good after so long in an airport? She probably smelled like dirty gym socks.

"Where you headed, Kelsey?" he asked, as if she wanted to have this conversation.

"Nowhere."

He looked surprised at the empty answer, and she winced. Shouldn't let her hopelessness stick out for everyone to see. The last thing she wanted was pity. She had enough of that for herself.

"Actually, I'm going to Dallas." She cast a doubtful eye at the huge observation windows. Sleet continued to ping against the panes. "Someday."

He grinned, and darn if he wasn't even better looking. She flat out hated him. "I know what you mean. We're going to Dallas, too."

She knew that. Everyone who could read knew Ryan Storm lived in, worked in and practically owned Dallas. Ryan Storm, businessman of the year, entrepreneur, most eligible bachelor. All the things she didn't like in a man.

Well, actually there was one more thing she didn't like in a man. Deceit. Mark had been so good at keeping her in the dark. And none of that was Ryan Storm's fault or his daughter's. It was her own fault for being so gullible, for wanting to believe.

The man of the year had turned to look at her during the conversation and suddenly his eyes narrowed. "I hope you won't take this the wrong way, but you look familiar. Have we met?"

She almost laughed. Did he realize how insulting that was? Not only did he not recognize her, he wanted to be sure she didn't mistake his question for interest in her as a woman. Like anyone would be interested in a pregnant cow who hadn't had a shower and shampoo since night before last.

"Bartlett High, Dallas east side, Mrs. Rutger's history class. Although you slept through most of it."

A flicker of recognition dawned behind an intense brown gaze. His mouth dropped open and he raised one finger in a struggle to remember her name. "Kelsey…Kelsey…" He snapped his fingers. "Kelsey Slater, boy hater."

The old nickname made Kelsey laugh. She hadn't really hated boys, but with braces, glasses and freckles, the oft-repeated comment served as ego protection. Guys liked her. They just didn't date her. The butterfly hadn't exited her cocoon until after high school. Contacts, straight teeth and the right makeup had done a world of wonders.

"It's Kelsey Mason now, but how did you remember that silly nickname?"

Expensive fabric whispered as Ryan lifted one wide shoulder. "A mind that never shuts off."

"You mean the way it did while your daughter was running around the airport alone?" She widened her eyes in horror. Had she really said that?

"Pardon?"

Apparently she had, and the man of the year hadn't taken it too well. "Never mind. None of my business."

Braces may have fixed her teeth but nothing had corrected her habit of saying what she thought. Sometimes her big mouth got her in trouble.

Mariah, who had been patiently taking in the conversation, tugged on her father's sleeve. "Daddy, please. You're interrupting our interview."

Ryan dragged his offended gaze from Kelsey to his daughter. "Sorry, peanut, but I don't think Kelsey would be interested in the position."

"But I think she might be *the one,* Daddy, although we haven't yet discussed credentions or salary."

"Credentials," he corrected.

Mariah nodded. Her curls bounced on the shoulder of a dark green jumper. "You can ask her about that."

"I don't think so. Married ladies usually aren't seeking nanny positions." He indicated Kelsey's left hand. "See? She has a wedding ring."

Boy, was he observant!

"Oh." The child looked betrayed as she spoke to Kelsey. "You didn't tell me you were married."

Kelsey twisted the ring, wondering why she bothered to wear it. For the baby, she supposed. Certainly not for any residual attachment to Mark. "I'm a widow. My husband died."

Saying the words aloud seemed as unreal now as they had a few months ago. Mark was dead, his body lost in a horrible explosion that sunk the extravagant yacht he was sailing to a buyer in Greece. She felt both horrified and guilty. Horrified that it happened. Guilty to feel so little grief.

Her expression must have shown the stress of the last few months, because Mariah's little hand took hers. "Don't be sad, Kelsey. Daddy and I will make you feel better. You can come to our house and have hot chocolate and graham crackers in bed." The bouncy curls swirled toward Ryan. "Can't she, Daddy? We'll make her feel better and she can look after me while you work. Then she can be my mommy and give me a baby sister. She's a teacher, too, so she can help us with our geography. I still get mixed up with India and Indiana, you know. It's the perfect solution."

Ryan appeared as muddled by his little girl's logic as Kelsey felt. After staring at the child for several beats, he ran his fingers across the top of his head in an exasperated manner. "You're a teacher? You wouldn't be needing a job, would you?"

He didn't know the half of it. "Exactly what kind of job?"

He gave a short laugh. "It's nothing quite as involved as Mariah has in mind. You see, Mariah's au pair has gotten married. We're on our way home from the wedding."

"And Miss Janine hasn't been replaced yet," Mariah said, folding both hands on Kelsey's kneecap and staring up into her face. "We interviewed a few candidates, but I have the final veto."

Her father rolled his eyes and looked pretty much helpless. "It's a deal we made. I choose qualifications. She chooses someone she likes. I work long hours and need someone I can totally trust with my child."

"Sometimes I don't see Daddy for days," Mariah said. "He works very, very hard, you know, and although I miss him terribly, I understand. People depend on him. That's why your credentions have to be exemplary. We'll be spending a lot of time together. I really want a baby sister. And I promise to be lots of help with her. I'll read all the baby books and learn everything. You won't have to worry one little bit. And I'm always well-behaved. I promise. Aren't I, Daddy?"

All during this long persuasive speech, Mariah's little face was a picture of hope. Kelsey's heart twisted. With each word, Kelsey had grown more sure that Ryan Storm was a success-oriented workaholic and not much else. Poor little Mariah.

"Yes, you are, peanut." Ryan tweaked the end of the little girl's nose and then spoke to Kelsey. "So you see, with Mariah's intellect, I need to hire someone who can not only care for her full-time, but who can homeschool her as Janine did. She didn't fit too well in kindergarten and I don't intend to expose her to that again."

"Kids in kindergarten didn't like me much, although I'll never understand their reasoning. Playing with blocks seemed a little silly to me, but I was still nice to them and helped them organize the blocks into a color-coordinated map of Dallas." Mariah frowned. "For some reason, that made them all run away."

Ryan tilted an eyebrow at Kelsey as if to say, see what I mean? "Private tutors, in my opinion, are best for children like Mariah."

"Eventually, she'll have to learn to interact with other children," Kelsey said. "No matter how bright she is, she needs to learn to play like a normal kid."

"I'm far more concerned with making the most of her intelligence. Kids are born knowing how to play."

"Well, I think you're wrong about that." Kelsey didn't know what possessed her, exhaustion she supposed, but she was still annoyed that the child had been running loose in the airport without supervision. Add to that Mariah's concern about her father's emotional well-being, and Kelsey figured the guy needed to get a clue. "Socialization is important, too, particularly at this age."

"My daughter is quite social, as you have already observed."

"That's not what I meant. Did it ever occur to you that she needs to be a little girl instead of worrying about you?" Oops. Now she'd gone too far.

He blinked, those intense eyes hardening to onyx. "Excuse me. I think this *interview* is concluded."

Well, la-dee-da. Concluded.

"And here I didn't even know an interview was going on. Silly me." Story of her life. Lose the job before she even applied for it. Before she could shove the next words back down her smart-aleck throat, she blurted, "Sounds like *somebody* needs a nap, and I don't mean your daughter."

After a tense ten seconds while her former classmate contemplated her with both surprise and curiosity and maybe even a little horror, he turned aside and stared out the frosted window.

Steepling his fingers, he bounced them against his chin with a sigh of utter hopelessness. For a fleeting moment, Ryan Storm, king of Storm International, looked like a lost child himself. Kelsey felt a twinge of sympathy, which made no sense under the circumstances. First of all she should be red-hot and furious at his dismissal, but she wasn't. She thought his defensive reaction was kind of funny and pompous and completely characteristic of the brooding young man she'd known in high school. He'd moved through the hallways with a know-it-all stare and a chip on his shoulder the size of Texas Stadium. Though he said little, his groupies followed, anxious to do the bidding of the rough-edged boy in fitted T-shirt and faded jeans. He was in command even then.

Secondly, and probably most important given the unpredictable state of her emotions, here was a man of enormous success and confidence who had the world in the palm of his hand. She, on the other hand, was a mess. Why should she feel sorry for Ryan Storm?

Mariah, who hadn't missed a single glare or sigh or comment, glanced from her father's stormy face to Kelsey's and back again. "Can't we negotiate?"

Worry filled her dark eyes and pinched Kelsey's conscience. Concern for her daddy emanated from her small form in pleading waves. Here was a child who could probably read Shakespeare but was stuck with a workaholic father who hadn't a clue. If ever a little girl needed a mommy, this one did.

"Didn't you hear? Kelsey isn't interested in the job," Ryan muttered.

Maybe it was the child's big brown eyes. Maybe it was the father's lost expression. Maybe it was hormones.

Most likely it was pure desperation.

"Actually," Kelsey said. "I think I am.

CHAPTER TWO

SLOWLY, SLOWLY, RYAN TURNED towards the woman. First, she'd told him he had no idea how to raise his own child. And now, she wanted to work for him.

He didn't think so.

He ran a hand down his face, heard the scratch of beard left untended.

Bone weary of sitting in this airport, he had missed two crucial meetings, and had just spent forty-five minutes on the telephone trying without success to salvage a deal gone sour. By the time he'd ended the call, Mariah had done one of her disappearing acts. His little girl was the only person on the planet who could ruffle his composure and send him into panic mode.

When he'd rounded the concourse and seen her here, talking to the pregnant woman, safe and sound, he'd nearly imploded with relief. If anything happened to Mariah, he couldn't go on. Losing Amanda had nearly killed him. Losing Mariah would.

As it was, she drove him crazy, her brilliant mind too young to make appropriate decisions and too smart not to explore the world around her. Once, she'd gotten away from Janine with a handful of change from his dresser and had boarded the trolley for a trip to the Dallas World Aquarium. A quick-thinking driver had saved them all a great deal of grief.

The child needed a keeper who was as smart as she.

Running on minimal sleep, he wasn't in the best frame of mind to make decisions. But Kelsey Slater, boy hater? Probably not.

All the reasons why he should not hire Kelsey loomed before him as obvious as her pregnant belly. That was the number one reason right there. Pregnant women made him nervous. No, not nervous. Terrified.

But she was someone he knew, at least had known. Kelsey had been the nice, ordinary girl in the front row whose hand was always in the air, volunteering to head the homecoming committee or to do cleanup after the dance. Only she looked so different. Really different. Her glasses had hidden the most stunning blue-green eyes he'd ever seen and a delicate, heart-shaped face framed by long, loose hair the color of his bedroom furniture. Mahogany. And he shouldn't be thinking of his bedroom in the same sentence with a nanny applicant.

Sheesh. He *was* tired.

"What makes you think you're right for the job?"

"What makes you think I'm not?"

The fact that I want to shut that sassy mouth of yours with a kiss.

For a horrified second, he thought he might have spoken aloud but when she didn't slap his face, he breathed a sigh of relief and said instead, "My daughter seems quite taken with you. Her needs are paramount."

"As they should be." She shifted uncomfortably. An airport was no place for a pregnant woman. She didn't look too far along, but her face and arms were thin, as if she'd recently lost weight instead of gaining. She could be about to pop for all he knew. A shudder of dread quivered up his spine and, in spite of the frigid temperatures, sweat broke out on his upper lip.

"I have a number of people to interview once we're back in Dallas. I'm sure I'll find someone suitable."

She gave him a look that said she questioned his sanity, a legitimate concern at the moment.

"Look, Ryan," Miss Pregnant and alone said. "Let me be honest here. I need a job and a place to live. I allowed my Texas teaching credentials to expire and even after I renew them, it's the middle of the term and I'm pregnant." She *would* have to bring that up again. "Finding a position isn't going to be easy."

No. She wouldn't do. He couldn't put himself through the agony of being reminded of those last days with Amanda.

"I'm an excellent teacher," Kelsey said. "And a good person who adores kids and knows how to get the best out of them. You know me, at least somewhat. That has to be a plus. I can do a good job for you and for Mariah."

He could read through an applicant's motives faster than gossip and Kelsey's were nothing short of desperation.

Sympathetic feelings had no place in business dealings, but he had to admit to having some. The Kelsey he remembered was a nice girl, almost too good, if talk among the guys was to be trusted. But hiring a nanny who could also homeschool his daughter in the manner he considered best was business. Purely business. If Kelsey had those qualifications—and she did—those were the only things that mattered. However, her attitude toward child-rearing was far different than his. He knew what was best for his daughter and if he hired Kelsey, she'd have to do things his way.

But he didn't want to hire her. She was pregnant. And a little too bossy. Nope, no way. No deal.

Then why couldn't he get past the lines of tension around her soft mouth or the worry in those stunning eyes? Why did he keep sitting here beside her, listening to the soft drawl in her voice and wondering what it would be like to have her in his employ, in his house?

"What about your family?" Surely, she was returning to Dallas to be with caring family members. Someone who could keep a close eye on her until the baby came.

Pink tinged the crest of her cheekbones. Any makeup she might have worn was long gone by now, and a smattering of freckles popped through the clear, lovely skin. The color of her hair, the fascinating freckles were like sprinkles of colored sugar on a bowl of cream.

Good lord, when had he become a poet? He really was too tired.

"My dad and stepmother still live in Dallas," Kelsey was saying, a little too stiffly. "But I'm not a charity case. I do not want to live off them or anyone else. I earn my way."

Ryan realized he had insulted her somehow. But in doing so, he'd discovered something important. For whatever reasons, Kelsey was down on her luck but she had a lot of pride. He'd been there, done that. Could completely relate. So much so that he admired the thrust of her chin and the glitter of pride in her eyes. She was stubborn, opinionated and pregnant. But she was also smart and qualified and someone he knew.

Mariah was right. They did need Kelsey Slater, boy hater. He'd interviewed half a dozen women already, but none that suited. On the other hand, none were pregnant former classmates who attracted him either. Everything in that sentence, other than the former classmate part, was not in Kelsey's favor.

Still, he needed to concentrate on his work, especially right now with the Toliver takeover on the horizon. Something about Kelsey annoyed and worried him as much as it attracted him— but maybe that could actually work to his advantage. He was gone sixteen hours a day or more anyway. No need to even see her or her pretty mouth or pregnant belly.

He shivered at the last thought. That was the deal breaker right there.

But his schedule next week was now doubled due to this airport delay. Given his aversion to day-care centers, he needed someone reliable—and fast.

If not for the pregnancy, Kelsey Slater, boy hater could fill the bill very well.

In high school, she'd been friendly to him even though he'd never run in her social circle. Truth was, his social circle had been on the outer edges, the group of boys and girls just shy of trouble. He'd been their leader, though most of his after-hours were spent working and trying to keep his family afloat. With a father who wandered in and out of his life at odd intervals, the role of man of the house had fallen to him most of the time. He'd worked his butt off, too, all the while plotting his way out.

His jaw tightened. He'd made it. With the sweat of his brow, unholy hours and a few unholy alliances he wasn't particularly proud of, he'd scratched his way to the top. By all that was good and right, he was going to stay there. Mariah would never know what it was like to come from the bottom of the barrel.

To keep his relentless work pace, he needed someone reliable to care for his daughter. He flicked another glance at the familiar woman with the blue-green eyes.

In his world, those who hesitated were lost. Deals could make or break on five minutes of indecision. He was known to make decisions quickly on gut instinct. So he swallowed down the last inner scream of protest and made one.

"You're hired."

* * *

Kelsey couldn't believe her ears. A gift horse had arrived upon the scene, literally falling from the sky. Did this mean the fickle finger of fate had decided to smile on her for a change?

"But I can't be."

Annoyance flashed on chiseled features. "Are we going to have this argument again?"

"Don't you want references? Shouldn't we discuss expectations and duties, days off and salary? You could be hiring a serial killer to care for your daughter." *Shut up, Kelsey. Shut up!*

Ryan raised a finger in silent command. Thank goodness. "You aren't a stranger. You just told me you were totally trustworthy and I believe you. And I'm a very good judge of character, as is Mariah."

Kelsey huffed. "Six-year-olds trust anyone with bubble gum or a puppy."

No wonder lady luck enjoyed tormenting her. She made it so easy.

Mariah came to life, face alight. "Do you have a puppy?"

"No honey, I don't." Kelsey ran a hand down the child's arm to soften the disappointment. Mariah had just made her point. "See what I mean?" she said to Ryan.

"You cheated. Even I'm a sucker for puppies."

She'd have to give him points for that. "But still, there are things to discuss."

"We can evaluate references and execute a contract once we're back in Dallas. If at that time the particulars don't suit one of us, we can, as Mariah says, negotiate."

And she knew who would come out on the short end of that stick. Her. Ryan had pulled himself out of poverty to multi-millionaire status. He hadn't gotten to the top of the heap on those stunning looks alone.

"You need a job. I need a nanny. Let's say a trial run. Thirty days. Deal or no deal?"

Who was she kidding? There was no way she could turn down his offer.

"Fine," she said. In her desperate state, she should be kissing his feet in gratitude. For the past five months, she'd held herself together with pride and spunk and not much else. When the cars and the house, the boats and the business all went on the auction block to pay off debts left by her late husband, Kelsey had gone from being the Mercedes-driving wife of a successful yacht dealer to being pregnant, alone and dead broke.

She should be grateful instead of argumentative. But she hated feeling obligated and something about Ryan Storm irritated her. Rubbing at tired eyes, she fought back tears. Resentment and despair welled in her. The baby reacted to her distress and fluttered around like an oversized butterfly. She laid a hand to the mound beneath her heavy sweater.

As if she'd slapped him, Ryan jerked, riveting his attention on her stomach. "Are you okay?"

"Sure." If she'd survived the last few months, she could survive being stranded in an airport.

Ryan swallowed. Kelsey wondered if the question had been deeper than a polite inquiry.

"Good. Good," he said. "You don't look fine. You look dead on your feet and stressed to the max."

"Thanks." Roadkill. She looked like roadkill.

"No insult meant."

"None taken." Yeah right.

"Mind if I ask what happened to your husband?"

The nightmare that had begun five months ago was never far from her thoughts. If she was going to work for this man, he needed to know.

She shook her head setting her hair into motion. It felt heavy and greasy against her scalp. What she wouldn't give for a shower and shampoo and a comfy bed.

"Mark was sailing a yacht to its new owner in Greece when something went wrong. An explosion of some kind. He was lost at sea."

"I'm sorry."

"Thank you." She never knew what else to say, though her answer sounded so unfeeling. It wasn't that she didn't feel terrible about Mark's death. It was that she was still so angry and bewildered at what he'd done.

"He was never found?"

One of the reasons the insurance company had refused to pay. No body, no money. A morbid prospect, she thought. "No. The investigation is ongoing but the Coast Guard insists no one could have survived the explosion and subsequent fire. There was nothing left of the yacht other than debris."

She'd heard the story and repeated the words so often to investigators, insurance adjusters, reporters and friends, but they still held that element of horror. No matter how she felt about Mark, she'd never wanted him dead.

The marriage had been rocky for so long that Kelsey was embarrassed to play the grieving widow. Still, hadn't she gotten pregnant in an attempt to draw them closer together? Foolhardy, she knew now because, instead of fixing the problem she'd made things worse. Mark had not been happy to add, as he called it, the financial burden of rearing a child to his busy life. She'd thought the notion ridiculous given how well they were doing financially. Or so she had thought.

Only after the accident did she discover some important details Mark had forgotten to mention. The business was in deep trouble. The money he took with him was all they had. He'd also put Mason Marine and all the accounts payable in her name. At first, she'd thought the action was sweet and loving—until reality dawned. Her husband had not left her the business as a means to care for her and their baby. He'd left her holding the bag.

A warm, masculine hand pressed against hers. Both Ryan and Mariah were studying her with concern. "Hey. You went a million miles away. Sorry to bring up such a painful topic."

She'd expected compassion from the child, but from Ryan? The man was as much as an enigma now as he'd been in high school.

How did she explain to him, or to anyone, that the greatest pain was not in losing a husband but in the knowledge that her husband hadn't really cared for her, or their child, at all?

She didn't. Her personal pain was her own.

"It's behind me now." A total lie. A mountain of debt and a string of bill collectors snapped at her heels like Doberman pinschers. Somehow, some way, she'd repay all that was owed.

He hitched an eyebrow in the direction of the soccer ball around her middle. "Not everything."

For the first time since Ryan Storm had stormed into her life in the middle of a snow storm, Kelsey felt a sense of calm at the mention of her pregnancy. However inconvenient the timing might be, her baby was the one joy, the one good thing, left in her life.

She stroked a protective hand over her belly. "Yes, there is the baby."

And she'd do whatever it took to make a good life for her unborn child.

"So is it a deal? You'll come to work for me? I promise you'll be well-compensated."

Well-compensated. She could deal with that. Here was a chance to save for the future, to pay off debts, to start over again for the sake of her child. What else could she say?

"A thirty-day trial?"

Ryan's smile was more dazzling than the Texas sun at high noon. He offered a hand. As his long, competent fingers encircled her slender hand, Kelsey experienced an array of emotions. Relief. Safety. And oh dear, a zing of physical attraction too strong to be ignored.

Ryan must have felt it, too, for he didn't turn loose of her hand for the longest time. Instead, he stared down at her with an intense and probing expression. Butterflies that had nothing to do with the baby fluttered in Kelsey's belly.

"Daddy, Kelsey, look," Mariah's little voice interrupted. The adults dropped their hands as if they'd held hot potatoes and turned toward the little girl. She pointed at the windows. "The snow stopped."

"So it has." As though nothing had passed between them, Ryan turned away from Kelsey and got up for a closer look.

Maybe the moment had been her wild imagination. Maybe it had been her fluxuating and unpredictable hormones. But she didn't think so.

The flutter intensified and she thought of her baby. This job was the best thing for him or her. And since Kelsey had no intention of ever getting romantic with a success-oriented workaholic like Ryan, she was perfectly safe. With that firmly in mind, she rose to follow Ryan and Mariah to the windows. Her cramped legs and back thanked her.

"The cloud cover seems to be breaking," Ryan was saying.

"It is, Daddy. See right there?" Nose pressed to the window, Mariah turned her face toward her father. Her expression was sweet and confident. "Just like I told you before. Everything will work out fine. And it has. We found Kelsey, and now the storm has stopped. Things are looking up."

Kelsey caught Ryan's eye and both adults chuckled.
Yes, indeed. Maybe things were finally looking up.
Even if Ryan Storm *was* a little too attractive.

CHAPTER THREE

MARIAH HAD BEEN RIGHT. Planes began to fly again in a matter of hours. Once their seats were secured, the newly formed trio trudged to an eatery for a late-night snack and a round of general conversation. In that hour, Kelsey began to feel far more comfortable with the idea of working for Ryan and tutoring Mariah. The child desperately needed a woman's influence and nurturing. And if there was one thing Kelsey could do, it was nurture.

The first sign of a snag came when Ryan said, "Before we board, I'll call ahead to be sure a car is available to take us home from the airport."

"I can get a cab." She poked a fork into her fruit cup, spearing a piece of melon. It was the only thing on the menu she could afford.

Ryan, who'd ordered a full country breakfast, paused in mid-bite, frown puzzled. The result of not shaving in a while framed his mouth in such a sexy manner, Kelsey could hardly stop staring. "Why would you need to do that?"

"It beats walking."

"You aren't walking. You're going home with us." The words were a statement of fact that brooked no argument.

Kelsey gulped, swallowing a whole grape. "You're kidding, right?"

"I hired you because I need you now. Tonight. Tomorrow."

The choice of words, coupled with his manly, scruffy look, brought to mind all kinds of possibilities. Troubling possibilities.

"I wasn't expecting to begin work quite this soon."

Nonchalantly, he applied grape jelly to his toast. The sound of knife against toast scraped against her nerves. "That was the deal."

Not the way Kelsey remembered. She shook her head. "I'd be a lunatic to go home with a strange man in the middle of the night."

"I'm not a stranger, Kelsey. You know me, and you have my assurance. You are perfectly safe with me and Mariah." He wiped a bit of ketchup from Mariah's chin. "Right, peanut?"

Mouth full of hamburger, Mariah batted her long-lashed eyes and bobbed her head at Kelsey in reassurance.

The little girl was such a sweetheart. Kelsey patted her hand and winked.

Though she'd been away from Dallas since her marriage four years ago, she still kept up with the local news. Ryan made the business news quite often and was known as a straight arrow who didn't party, much to the dismay of Dallas society. And he had a child, for goodness sake.

"But my family is expecting me." Sort of.

"Call them."

"At this time of night?"

He gestured with his fork. "Either way, you'll wake them."

The man had an answer for every argument. "Now I understand how you became successful at such an early age."

He grinned. Her stomach dipped so that she almost backed out of the entire deal.

But in the end, her desperate need for a job and a place to live, along with Ryan's quiet insistence, won out and she agreed to go straight to his home. As a last-ditch effort at common sense, she'd phoned her father to let him know her whereabouts. He'd been none too happy about the late call, so she'd been brief, promising to drop by as soon as she was settled in her new job. Jim Slater had mumbled, "Fine," and hung up. It was no more than Kelsey had expected. Relations had been strained since her father remarried so soon after her mother's death.

Still, she felt strange following Ryan Storm around the airport, through the terminal and into the waiting limo.

The sensation didn't improve upon arriving at his upscale, two-story town house in east Dallas.

Ryan, on the other hand, behaved as though he brought strange women home all the time. The thought gave Kelsey pause. Maybe he did. Maybe he was just ultra sneaky about it.

With Mariah draped across his shoulder asleep, he nudged his chin toward the stairs. "Second door on the right."

Kelsey went ahead of him, flipped on the light and stripped the covers back on the canopy bed in preparation for the slumbering child. Ryan smiled his thanks and slid his small, limp load between the pink princess sheets.

"Shall I undress her?" Kelsey asked but didn't wait for an answer. She reached for the child's shoes while Ryan stripped away her coat.

"Good enough for tonight," he said quietly. "Let her sleep."

In the hush, she watched him tuck the cover beneath the sleeping beauty before placing a kiss on her forehead. Mariah squirmed, mumbled and then flopped over, burrowing deeper into the soft, inviting bed.

Tenderness crept into Ryan's exhausted face. He stood beside the bed, looking down at his child for several long, sweet seconds. Emotion fluttered beneath Kelsey's ribcage as she wondered about the man who was never home but who appeared to adore his child. Was he simply unaware of how much his child needed him? Or was he, like Mark, more concerned with success than with his family?

She also wondered about Mariah's mother. What kind of tragedy had taken her at such a young age? What kind of woman was she that a man like Ryan Storm had married her? Did he still love her? How well had Mariah dealt with her mother's loss?

Straightening, Ryan snapped off the bedside lamp, plunging the room into semidarkness. The resulting atmosphere was softly intimate, too much so. With a tilt of his head Ryan motioned toward the door. They brushed arms in the doorway and Ryan stepped back, letting her pass first. The air between them trembled with the same something she'd felt in the airport when their hands had touched.

"This way," he murmured, gesturing to the left. "Your room will be this one next to Mariah's if it suits."

"I'm sure it will." Right now, she just wanted someplace to lie down and put her feet up. And a shower. Oh, a shower would be heaven.

"I'll bring your bags up in a minute."

"I can get them."

As if she'd threatened to burn the house down, Ryan spun around, jaw tight, eyes blazing. His mood had gone from tender to angry.

"You will not carry bags upstairs. You will not even carry grocery bags from the car to the house. Nor will you lift anything heavy while in my employ. Ever. Understand?"

Kelsey took one step back, surprised at the intensity of the remark. Was this guy moody or what?

"I'd be pretty stupid not to," she snapped. "Although I see no need for you to be cranky about it."

Ryan said nothing else, but his odd mood quivered in the air.

Pushing a door open, he motioned her inside. Still miffed by his sharp comments, she brushed past him, but the move was too close for comfort. As in the airport, she caught the scent of expensive male cologne, glanced the surprisingly muscled arm stretched flat across the raise-paneled door. He still hadn't shaved and his shirt—unbuttoned at the collar, his tie long ago stuffed into a pocket—was coming untucked. The result was bedroom sexy and deliciously rumpled.

Darn. There she went again.

Living under the same roof with a man who caused her mind to think such things might not be such a smart move. But it was done. At least for thirty days.

"It's lovely," she said when they entered the bedroom. A small sitting area, complete with desk, chair and television opened into a bed and bath. Sleek, elegant and modern with mint-green walls and cream trim, it was generically right for a guest or an employee of status.

The room was as beautiful as any she'd ever seen, but Kelsey felt oddly disappointed. A lump of loneliness rose in her throat. She and her baby had no home to call their own. All her dreams of decorating a nursery, buying the perfect furniture and giving her baby everything tormented her. The only thing she could give her baby now was love.

She must have looked as lost as she felt because Ryan touched her shoulder. She glanced up, saw the mood had changed again. "You're dead on your feet. Go to bed."

At the unexpected kindness, tears burned the back of her eyes. "I have to take a shower first."

He remained there, staring at her for several seconds. "You'll be okay here?"

She swallowed back the troublesome emotions and forced a cheeky grin. "Sure I will. You promised not to murder me."

The corner of Ryan's mouth quirked. "If you need anything tonight—"

"I won't. Go to bed, Ryan. You're as tired as I am." And if he stood around any longer, she might cry and embarrass them both.

"But I'm not pregnant." The comment was an accusation, as though he resented the fact that he'd hired a pregnant nanny.

"It isn't a terminal disease," she said.

As though she'd slapped him, Ryan recoiled. Behind the outline of dark beard, his natural tan drained away. For a moment he wrestled with something. His mouth opened and closed. His chest rose and fell. And then without another word, he whipped around and left the room.

But not before Kelsey saw the misery in his eyes.

"Kelsey, wake up."

Kelsey awakened in a strange room, disoriented. She lay very still, moving only her eyes until they focused on Mariah perched cross-legged next to her, books spread about her in a circle. The cobwebs cleared. She'd thought it was a dream, but she was really here, in the home of Ryan Storm. Memory came flooding in. In some moment of insanity she'd agreed to work for a man she barely knew.

Okay, so she'd been attracted to him. What woman on planet Earth, pregnant or not, wouldn't be? And she'd been flattered at the instant trust he'd placed in her. After all, he was Ryan Storm, king of Dallas. Able to buy tall buildings with a single check.

Taking the position was a good thing, she'd told herself last night as she'd stood beneath the rain showerhead, washing hours of stomach-churning airport smells down the drain. She had a paying job, and both she and the baby had a place to live. At least temporarily.

She just wished she didn't feel so weird about it.

Small fingers patted her knee. "Good morning. Are you awake yet?"

Then there was the other reason she'd agreed to come here. Mariah. The brilliant child who had touched her heart in Denver.

"Good morning," she muttered after clearing the gravel from her throat. She stretched and looked around for a clock. An Asian-influenced wall hanging, more art than clock, read seven o'clock. Kelsey stifled a groan. Five hours of sleep to a pregnant woman was next to none.

"I hear Daddy downstairs," Mariah said, raising up on her knees. "If we want to see him, we'll have to hurry. He's a very busy man."

Kelsey's heart squeezed. The little girl must have gotten up some time ago to bathe and dress herself in anticipation of spending time with her dad. Except for the mismatched colors, she appeared to have done a good job, fully dressed in a purple hoodie and green sweat pants. Her natural curls, still damp from a shampoo, had been ruthlessly stripped back from her face with a red headband.

Kelsey patted the child's knee. "I doubt he'll leave until we've had an opportunity to work out the conditions of my nannyship."

Mariah giggled, putting both hands over her mouth in that adorable manner. "That's a good one. Nannyship. Is it a real word I should add to my lexicon?"

A six year old with a lexicon? Good heavens. Kelsey shook her head and sat up. Sumptuous ivory sheets slid over her shoulders and pooled in her lap. "Not real, but real fun."

"Should I leave so you can get dressed? Or would you like to begin my classes now? I brought in some of my books."

"I thought you wanted to see your father."

"I do, but he always says we must prioritize. Important things like work and education come first."

"Seeing your dad is important, too." Kelsey threw the covers back and swung her feet over the side of the bed. She dug her toes into the soft rug. "You go on and say good morning. I'll be down shortly."

The child scrambled off the bed and rushed to the door before turning back.

"I think your nannyship is going to work out perfectly," Mariah said, grinning, and then she bounced through the door and disappeared.

Kelsey hoped the little optimist was right.

By the time she dressed and descended the stairs, Ryan and Mariah sat at a small table in the breakfast room pouring over a computer-generated document. They were so engrossed that neither heard her soft footsteps on the stone-tiled kitchen floor.

A weak winter sun spilled through French doors and gleamed on the two dark heads bent close together. Mariah's face was a study in attentiveness, soaking up the attention from her daddy. Ryan was in profile, his angled jaw free from the stubble of last night, his firm, sensual lips in motion. His mouth fascinated her and she tried hard not to imagine that he was probably a dynamite kisser. When the corners tipped up to smile at his daughter, she nearly swooned. Gone was any hint of the despair she'd imagined last night. Exhaustion and imagination could be the only sensible explanation for Ryan's odd reaction to her silly comment about pregnancy.

Gone, too, was last night's deliciously rumpled traveler. This morning he looked polished and professional. Unfortunately, he also looked every bit as yummy.

She felt like the governess mooning over the lord of the manor in one of those gothic novels. A most disconcerting flutter of awareness invaded Kelsey's being. That would not do. It would not do at all. Wasn't she supposed to be immune to good-looking, successful men after what happened with Mark?

As if he felt her stares, Ryan glanced up. The remnant of his smile was still in place. She smiled back, fighting a blush because of her wayward thoughts.

"Good morning. I see you survived the night." Amusement danced in his eyes. She wrinkled her nose at him and he laughed. "There's fresh coffee in the carafe if you'd like some."

With a shake of her head, Kelsey touched her tummy. "No thank you."

Though she was long past morning sickness, her stomach had tangled into a thousands knots. Might as well face it. She'd have to be very careful around Ryan Storm. Something about him disturbed her in a dangerously elemental way. To make matters worse, she felt obligated to him. Neither feeling sat well. But she also firmly believed Mariah needed her, and right now, Kelsey needed to be needed. She and her baby also needed this job.

"Join us then," Ryan said, pulling out a chair next to his. "I'd like to get things settled quickly and get to the office."

"You're going in to your office this morning?" She'd expected him to stick around and observe her with Mariah today.

"Daddy's time is very valuable," Mariah said gravely.

Well, so was everyone's. Wasn't time with his child valuable, too? His attitude wiped away any thoughts of how hot he was.

"I've already checked your references, which are excellent by the way."

"I knew that," she groused. The fact that he was up early after minimal sleep, checking references and looking so good added to her irritation. She still felt like roadkill and probably looked worse.

Ryan didn't seem to notice. He pushed the computer printout toward her. "Mariah and I were going over the list of duties and responsibilities. I'll leave those for you to look over. If you have any questions, my office number is there as well as my private cell. Do not give that to anyone."

As if she would.

"Here's Mariah's schedule."

"Schedule?"

"Janine worked out a schedule of study so Mariah could make the most of her time."

Kelsey had a feeling she and Janine would not have gotten along. "But she's only six. Why don't you let us play it by ear for a few days and then decide exactly what course of action we want to take?"

"I want her educated, Kelsey. That's why I hired a teacher. Just stick to the schedule and we'll get along fine." The words were mild, but the meaning was tempered with steel. She was not to question his authority. And she shouldn't, of course. Mariah was his child.

"Okay. I can do that." She hoped.

"I've also left full instructions about the alarm system and other household concerns. A housekeeper comes in daily. She'll prepare lunch, take care of the house and prepare dinner before leaving. Her name is Abilena Rueda. How's your Spanish?"

"Poor to nonexistent."

"Abilena understands a bit of English, but if you need her to do something, tell Mariah. Her Spanish is coming along fairly well."

"Daddy bought me some CDs," Mariah said proudly. "Acquiring a foreign language has become a necessity in today's global market. Isn't that right, Daddy?"

Ryan got that helpless look on his face again. The one that said Mariah's intellect both pleased and frightened him. "That's right, peanut. Knowledge is power."

Returning his attention to Kelsey, he pointed to a number on one of the sheets of paper. "Is the salary sufficient?"

Kelsey squinted, her contacts still a little watery. When the numbers focused in, she gasped. "Sufficient? Ryan, with this amount I can begin to pay off some of my—" She caught herself in time to keep from blurting out the painful truth of her finances.

But Ryan was every bit as bright as his child. His gaze narrowed as he studied her face. "If you need money just say so. Finances are not a problem here."

Heat rushed up the back of her neck. Money didn't used to be a problem with her either, but times change. "I can take care of it."

"I want your focus on teaching Mariah, not on worrying about finances. If you need money, tell me."

Humiliated but also grateful, she said, "That's kind of you, Ryan. Really. But I can handle it."

"Sure?" He seemed sincerely concerned.

"I have some old debts from the move. No big deal. Don't worry. I have everything under control." Right, and she could run the Boston marathon in five minutes in high heels.

"All right. If you need anything, all you have to do is ask." He took another sip of his coffee and pushed away from the table to slip into his jacket. "I'll see you lovely ladies later." He glanced at his daughter. "That's called alliteration—lovely ladies later."

"Alliteration." Mariah savored the word on her tongue as if it was good chocolate.

"Kelsey can teach you more about that."

"Cool." Mariah hopped down from her chair and followed him through the kitchen, through the foyer to the front door where he crouched down for a hug.

Kelsey had followed the pair, though she didn't know why, and the sweet moment between father and daughter squeezed her heart. He might be clueless, but Ryan appeared to be a caring daddy.

Three days later, as she checked Mariah's schedule, Kelsey was having second thoughts about Ryan Storm's parenting skills. It was six o'clock and the man had not yet appeared. Again. And the child was still studying as if she were taking the bar exam in the morning.

By now, their schedule was practically memorized and Mariah knew it better than Kelsey did. After all, Miss Janine, who Kelsey did not like at all, had manufactured this form of child torture some time ago. Mariah seldom complained, but an occasional sigh told the tale. Janine's regimented, unimaginative idea of educating a small child took a toll, both on the teacher and the student. Kelsey, who loved teaching, had never been so bored in her life.

"I think this is about it for the evening, don't you, sweetie?" she asked, gently closing the ancient-history book. "How about a game before bedtime?"

"Chess?" Mariah asked.

Kelsey thought if she lost another game of chess this week she'd die of humiliation. "How about something else? I think my brain needs a rest. How about—" She looked around for ideas.

"Monopoly? I'm really good at that."

Kelsey laughed. "I'll bet you are. Another tycoon in the making."

But she got the game out anyway, as eager for some fun as the child.

They were in Mariah's muted blue playroom which was more of an office than a fun place to hang out. The chest full of toys and games wasn't opened until recess which occurred three times a day—fifteen minutes in the morning, immediately following lunch and mid-afternoon. The rest of the time was spent in study. After dinner each evening, Mariah could read or play educational games before an early bedtime. From morning until night, every minute of Mariah's day was regimented as strictly as the military, which meant Kelsey's day was, as well. No shopping excursions. No visits with neighbors. No opportunity to get reacquainted with her beloved native city.

Frankly, she was suffocating.

To make matters worse, she'd seen Ryan only once, for less than an hour, and Mariah hadn't seen her father at all. The man was a workaholic to the extreme. He rose before either she or Mariah and returned long after Mariah, and sometimes she, had retired for the night. When he was at home, he disappeared into his office with a plate of food left by Abilena, not to be seen again that evening.

Several times each day, he phoned to check on Mariah, but the calls were brief and to the point. "How are things going? Good. Need anything? No? Bye."

Mariah, bless her little heart, was a trooper about her father's apparent indifference. Kelsey's thoughts were not so generous.

During the Monopoly game, Mariah paused time and again to listen for the garage door opening, the hope in her expression apparent.

"Do you think Daddy will be here to tuck me in tonight?" she said, adding a hotel to Boardwalk.

"He'll have to hurry. It's time for your bath now."

"What about our game?"

"Let's leave it to finish another time."

Mariah looked doubtful. "Janine never let me leave things out. She said I had to learn the importance of taking care of my possessions and not to take things for granted even if my daddy is rich."

Though the statement carried some truth, the manner in which it was said rankled. Had Janine been jealous of this child?

"Tell you what. You get your bath. I'll put the game in a safe place and then we'll snuggle up and read in bed for a while. Deal?"

Snuggle time was fast becoming a part of their routine that both of them enjoyed.

"Deal!" Mariah's brown eyes danced as she skipped off to the bathroom.

After straightening the play room, Kelsey slipped into her

robe and rejoined the sweet-smelling, freshly bathed child. Mariah was already in bed, her dark hair curled into squiggles across the pale pink pillowcase.

Intentionally choosing a simple, silly, rhyming Dr. Seuss book, Kelsey joined her. Together they giggled and snuggled, talked and made up stories.

When Mariah began to yawn and her eyelashes drooped for the third time, Kelsey pulled her close for a hug. She smelled of soap and shampoo and the cool essence of childhood.

"Time for lights out, precious."

Mariah cast a longing look toward the doorway. "I guess Daddy got stuck at the office," she said trying to rationalize why her father had not arrived. "He's a very busy man."

"Would you like to give him a call? Tell him goodnight? I'm sure he'd like that." She wasn't sure of any such thing, but she could hardly bear the disappointment wafting in waves from Mariah.

At the eagerness in the child's face, Kelsey reached for the telephone.

Ryan answered the cell phone on the third ring. "Is something wrong?"

"Mariah wants to say goodnight."

"Oh. Sure. Put her on." He sounded distracted. Not that she cared. Mariah was more important than whatever he found to do at this time of night.

The father and daughter spoke for a couple of minutes. All the while, Kelsey watched Mariah's face, listening to her sweet chatter, her delighted giggle at something Ryan said, and finally the wistful "I love you, Daddy" before returning the phone to Kelsey and snuggling down onto the pillow.

"He's nice," she said with a smile before letting her eyes flutter closed against soft, round cheeks.

Kelsey thought her heart would crack right in half.

Mariah had no mother and an absent father. She had no friends or doting relatives that Kelsey had seen. Mariah Storm was truly a poor little rich girl. And her father didn't have sense enough to see a problem. Either that or Mariah was an afterthought, a responsibility and nothing more.

It was time to have a little heart-to-heart with the man of the year. And he probably wasn't going to like it one bit.

CHAPTER FOUR

DOG TIRED, RYAN TOSSED his jacket and tie over a chair as he entered the town house, eager to flop down for an hour or so in front of the tube and think about nothing. The house was quiet and dark, as it always was when he arrived home. Only the hum of the refrigerator and the snick of the heating unit broke the silence. Mariah would be asleep by now. He'd sneak in later and grab a kiss.

The nanny must have gone to bed early, too. At nearly six months along, she probably tired easily. Amanda had.

He dashed that train of thought immediately and poured a glass of wine, his only concession to relaxation other than workouts in the basement of the office building. A gym for employees was one of the perks of working for Storm International. Healthy bodies translated to healthier work habits, better production and fewer sick days.

Kicking off his shoes, Ryan collapsed in the overstuffed leather chair and pointed the remote. As a kid, he'd dreamed of the day he could say he was a millionaire. Others had erroneously considered him rebellious or lazy, but he'd been plotting the future, figuring angles and working his tail off while others slept.

Lord, he was tired. But a man didn't stay on top without working sixteen hour days. One slip and he'd be back in the slums again, grubbing for every dollar. The mere thought of returning to those days spurred him to work harder and harder. He would never allow Mariah to live the way he had as a youth.

Setting his glass on the hexagonal table, he leaned his elbows on his knees and scrubbed both hands over his face. Maybe he should go on to bed. His day started early.

"Ryan."

At the soft voice, he jerked his head up. Kelsey stood in the wide entry of the living room. He hadn't heard her come down the stairs. She wore a long blue robe of some soft-looking fuzzy material that covered her from neck to toe and turned her eyes aquarium blue. In the loose, flowing garment, her pregnancy was hardly noticeable.

"Hi. I thought you were in bed by now."

She smiled and moved into the room, taking a seat on the couch across from him. After slipping off a pair of slip-on house shoes, she curled her feet beneath her.

Ryan's stomach dipped at the pleasantly domestic sight. In the faded light of one small lamp, Kelsey looked pretty and soft and vulnerable. Forcing his gaze away, he reached for the wine glass.

Ryan Storm had a hard and fast policy never to get personally involved with an employee. Never, never, never mix business with pleasure. And yes, after a very long day of haggling and dealing, looking at Kelsey was pure pleasure. But he'd seen too many CEOs fall to the wayside over a pretty assistant.

Trouble was, he also had a policy never to hire a beautiful woman to work in his house. Janine had been hired in part because she was older and matronly. He'd never expected the woman, who seldom left the house, to find husband number three and move away. He was still puzzled about that turn of events.

What had he been thinking the night he'd insisted on bringing Kelsey home with him? She was pretty *and* pregnant. Good grief. He was an idiot.

"I need to talk to you about something."

Her mahogany hair was swept away from her forehead and clipped with a tortoiseshell barrette. Straight and simple, her hair fell to her shoulders, gleaming in the lamplight as she moved. Her pale skin was scrubbed clean so that she looked fresh and young and innocent. If he breathed deeply, he was certain to catch the scent of fragrant soap and shampoo.

He would not allow himself that luxurious temptation. "Shoot."

She made a huffing sound. "Don't tempt me."

Puzzled, he tilted back in his chair. "Sorry. Did I miss something?"

"Constantly."

No matter how lovely she looked, the woman was talking in riddles. A straight-shooter, riddles always annoyed him. "Look, Kelsey, I've had a long day. Could we have this conversation another time?"

With a sarcastic curl of her lip she said, "Should I make an appointment with your secretary?"

The nanny was getting testy and he had no idea why.

"Is there a problem with Mariah?" He took a bigger sip of wine. Chardonnay. Lovely stuff. He took another.

"She misses you."

"I miss her." He swirled the lovely wine round and round staring into the depths.

"Then come home earlier. Spend some time with her."

"In case it's slipped past you, I run a very large company. Time is money. If I'm not there when a deal happens, it's gone." Why was he explaining this to her? "You were hired to spend time with my daughter. If she's lacking anything, I expect you to take care of it."

She cocked her head and looked at him as if he were a specimen in a laboratory. He couldn't help noticing how pretty her finely arched eyebrows were, even if they were raised mockingly at him.

"You don't have clue, do you?"

Now that statement annoyed him. He was not in the habit of being dressed down by employees, no matter how attractive their eyebrows. "Need I remind you that I'm her father and you're an employee. Of less than a week. An employee here on a trial basis."

He wasn't sure why he'd thrust that last, unnecessary jab. Nonetheless, a change shifted across Kelsey's placid features. Fear? Uncertainty? If he'd been in a business meeting he would have rejoiced at the victory. With Kelsey, he felt like a jerk.

"You're right, of course." Her voice was as mild and sweet as vanilla pudding but those startling blue-green eyes snapped. "I *am* an employee. So, let's get down to business, Mr. Storm."

Uh-oh, he'd made the nanny angry. Good. Better than having her afraid. This was the airport Kelsey, the one who'd taken him to task and come out a winner. He admired her feisty side.

A tiny smile took root in his chest, but he fought it down, figuring Kelsey would not take kindly if he grinned at her right now. "Go ahead. I'm listening."

"First of all, I'm concerned about Mariah's lack of interaction with others. Have you considered enrolling her in some day camps or other extracurricular activities?"

"Miss Janine wasn't much on extracurricular." Driving around in the city scared the woman mindless.

"I'm not Miss Janine."

"So I'd noticed." *Really* noticed.

"Would you mind if I take Mariah on some educational outings and look into the possibility of a day camp of some kind?"

"As long as you make the most of her education. Teaching is why you're here."

"I understand that. But the curriculum…" She sucked her bottom lip between her teeth and looked off toward the darkened kitchen. Ryan looked at her bottom lip.

"What's wrong with the curriculum? It's supposed to be the best there is."

"The books are fine, if a little long on reading and short on creative expression."

He frowned. Creativity in his world was essential. The creative ones, those who could think outside the box, were the ones who went somewhere. Guys like him. "I'm all for creative expression as long as educational value is the focus."

Suddenly she smiled, and Ryan forgot what he was about to say.

"Thank you, Ryan." She unwound her long legs from the couch and stood, lithe and smooth, the baby around her middle not yet slowing her down. "I'll go to bed now."

He felt as though he'd missed something in their conversation, but for the life of him he couldn't figure out what it was.

She started across the room but paused in the arched entryway and swiveled, the robe flowing out around her as if she were royalty. Back in high school, in comparison to him, she had been. Funny how life changed. He was the boss now, the one in command. Yet sometimes he still felt like that back-alley kid.

"What?" he asked.

She stood for a moment as though making a decision. A master at negotiations, he waited her out. If it was important enough, she'd say it. Finally, her soft voice said, "Could I ask a favor of you?"

A question like that was always a trap. People asking for favors, donations, jobs for relatives and on and on. At the office, he had full-time staff to field such requests. But those staff members were not here tonight, and in truth, he didn't feel at all defensive. Maybe she needed more money. More time off. Certainly more of something. They always did. But he could handle a nanny.

"What is it?"

"Would you please come home tomorrow before Mariah's bedtime?"

He stared at her for several seconds, trying to comprehend the request. "That's all you want?"

Wry amusement lifted the corners of her soft mouth. "It seems to be a rather big deal to one little girl I know."

Mentally, he reviewed tomorrow's calendar. Getting home at a decent hour would be tight.

"Tell Mariah I'll try to make it. No promises, but I'll give it my best shot."

Her smile was worth the sacrifice. "You're going to love snuggle time."

And then she swept out of the room, her feet tapping lightly as she ran up the stairs.

Ryan stood listening for the snap of her bedroom door. Then he tossed back the last of his wine and smiled into the semi-darkness.

What the heck was snuggle time?

Kelsey woke up the next morning feeling pretty proud of herself. Ryan had agreed with every single request. Maybe he wasn't as much of a know-it-all as she'd thought. An intensely driven man like Ryan didn't want theory. He wanted action. Once he saw how well Mariah responded to more peer interaction and innovative methods of stimulating her brilliant mind, he'd be all for it. She hoped.

Right now, Mariah most needed a friend around her age.

Once that was accomplished, Kelsey could take Mariah's dry curriculum and figure out ways to interject a little more fun.

Following a number of phone calls, she enrolled Mariah in a local homeschool network's playgroup three hours a week and jotted down a half dozen other places to go and things to do. The action wasn't all that earth-shattering, but it was a start and Mariah seemed taken with the idea.

She was also taken with the idea of spending some quality time with her father. In fact, she talked of little else as evening approached.

"Did Daddy say what time he'd be here?" Mariah asked for at least the tenth time. No matter how many times Kelsey answered, the child was fixated on the question.

"Remember what I told you," Kelsey warned. "He's going to try, but he didn't promise."

She would personally strangle the man if he did not show up on time.

"He'll be here. I just know it."

Kelsey certainly hoped so.

Later that afternoon, after a morning of grueling study, Kelsey had to get out of the house or throw-up. Abilena, the wonderful housekeeper, had come and gone, leaving a casserole for dinner. The Tex-Mex smells, usually welcome, bothered Kelsey today. That was the funny thing about pregnancy. One day she could eat her weight in food and the next day nothing sounded appealing.

"What about my homework?"

"It'll still be there when we return. I need some fresh air."

"Because you're having a baby?"

Was her queasiness that obvious? Kelsey touched her belly and smiled. "Yes, and also because everyone needs some fresh air, even in the winter."

They walked to the park which was only a few blocks away. The day was mild, if a bit gray and breezy, as winter in Dallas often is, requiring only hooded sweatshirts. For a woman accustomed to physical activity, Kelsey was glad for the opportunity to stretch her legs. Mariah skipped ahead, singing rhymes and taking care not to step on the cracks.

Kelsey recited the familiar schoolyard chant. "Step on a crack. You'll break your mother's back."

Mariah stopped and spun around. "I don't have a mother."

"Sure you do, sweetheart. But she's in heaven." This was one topic they had yet to explore.

"Your husband, too," she answered. "Does it still make you sad?"

"Sometimes. How about you?" Neither Mariah nor Ryan had offered to discuss how Mariah's mother had died. Though curious, Kelsey wouldn't pry, especially from a child.

Mariah contemplated the question before nodding. "I was really small. Does it hurt to have a baby?"

Well, if that wasn't a good indicator that Mariah had no wish to discuss her mother, she didn't know what was.

"I'm not sure. I've never had a baby before."

"Oh." The answer must have stumped her. Kelsey could see the wheels turning in the bright little head but had no way of knowing what the child was thinking. Given the topic, she felt it best not to ask. Somehow, she knew Ryan would not want her to discuss childbirth with his six-year-old.

By now, they'd reached the park and Mariah dashed off to the swings. Kelsey followed, drawing in the sweet scent of fresh air. She pushed Mariah for a while, relished her joyous laughter. The wind blew her black hair into tangles and reddened her round cheeks, but she was having too good a time to leave. After a bit, Kelsey joined her, swinging in the mindless rhythm of relaxation.

Coming here to work for Ryan Storm was a godsend. With Mariah to occupy her mind and time, she'd stopped worrying so much about the mountain of debt and the haggles with the insurance company. Tomorrow she had a doctor's appointment, the first with her new obstetrician. Other than stress, she was fine and her Seattle doctor had declared her fit during a checkup two weeks ago.

The baby was one topic she hadn't discussed much with Ryan. Would he allow her to continue her work after the baby came? She hoped so. She'd always dreamed of being a stay-at-home mom, at least until her kids started school.

Kids. A sadness tugged beneath her breastbone. Mark hadn't wanted any. She'd wanted several. How sad to realize after his death that they'd never really known each other at all.

The sounds of the city ebbed and flowed around them. Buses pulled to a stop across the street, their airbrakes hissing. Several people, including a woman with two small children, exited one of the buses. The petite blonde, holding the hands of a boy and girl who looked near to Mariah's age, brought them onto the playground.

"That's Mrs. Clonts with Chelsea and Tristan. They live in the condo down the street from us."

"They do?"

"Yes. Next door to the Bryants. I know all the neighbors. Daddy made a diagram of the area for me in case I ever get lost, which I never will, but it seemed to soothe him to do it, so I let him." Mariah hopped down from the swing. "I'll introduce you."

And she did. Following introductions, the Clonts children shot away to climb a wooden fort. Mariah, after hanging back with the adults for several minutes, couldn't resist the squeals of laughter as Tristan chased his sister up the ladder yelling something about pirates and fair maidens.

With a painfully adult-like stiffness, Mariah said, "I really like reading about pirates. They're very interesting."

"Wouldn't you rather pretend to be a pirate for a change?" Kelsey asked gently, a hand on Mariah's straight back.

"It does sound ever so fun."

"Yes, it does." With a gentle nudge, she urged Mariah toward the squealing kids. "Go on."

A sense of satisfaction settled over Kelsey when her little charge trotted toward the brother and sister. The child needed this far more than she needed to sit in her room studying.

While the children played, Kelsey also made a new acquaintance in Tammy Clonts. The neighbor was friendly and talkative—just what Kelsey needed after days in the company of only a six-year-old and dear Abilena who spoke little English.

Since coming back to Dallas, she hadn't contacted any of her old friends. She wanted to, but she wasn't yet up to explaining the nightmare of the last few months. The same was true of her family. They'd spoken by phone, but Dad had his own life now that wouldn't welcome her problems.

"So you're Ryan Storm's new nanny," Tammy said as they settled on a park bench. "I didn't expect someone as pretty and young as you."

Kelsey's surprise must have shown because Tammy laughed. "Sorry. Don't mind me. I have an alligator mouth. For Mariah's sake I'm glad you're young. That Janine was about as much fun as a drill sergeant."

Kelsey grinned. "Since I've been trying to follow the schedule she devised for Mariah, I tend to agree. Did you know her well?"

"Not really. She didn't like to socialize much. But Mr. Storm had a huge birthday party last year for Mariah and invited my kids. All the kids in the neighborhood, actually. Janine looked as though she'd swallowed a bug the whole time. I don't think she liked having all those noisy kids underfoot."

"Was Ryan there?" The idea that Ryan had given a party for Mariah warmed Kelsey's heart. Maybe he was more attuned to his daughter's needs than she gave him credit for.

"Oh, sure, he was there. He had a ball playing along with the magician he'd hired to entertain. It was kind of fun seeing a big time CEO pulling quarters out of kids' ears."

Kelsey smiled at the image. Ryan playful? She'd never seen that side of him. Even in high school, he'd always been so intense.

"Does he socialize much?"

The blonde glanced up, humor dancing in her brown eyes. "You mean with us neighbors? Or with women?"

Kelsey fought back a blush. Okay, so she was curious.

"With anyone."

"He's sort of an enigma, even to his neighbors. Really quiet and private. I'm sure you know more about him than we do."

The comment was an obvious hint for information but Kelsey already felt guilty enough for saying anything. "I guess I shouldn't gossip about my employer."

"Well, darn," Tammy said with good nature. They both laughed and Kelsey was relieved when Tammy didn't pry further. She couldn't afford to lose this job and she was most certain Ryan would not appreciate being the topic of her conversation with a neighbor.

The talk turned to the children and then quite naturally moved on to Kelsey's pregnancy. Tammy was full of advice about formulas, diapers and childbirth.

When the time came to leave, the group started off together on foot, leaving the bus ride for another time. In truth, Kelsey didn't want to spend even one cent on anything unnecessary.

As they crossed the street, sirens wailed in the distance. Fire trucks, maybe. She paid little attention to the sound, other than to register more than one. Sirens in the city were the norm.

When they reached the town house, Kelsey felt refreshed and energized. The fading sirens were the last thing on her mind.

CHAPTER FIVE

"COULD I STAY UP A LITTLE longer? Please. Daddy will be here soon. I just know it."

Eight-thirty had come and gone. Kelsey lay with Mariah snuggled under her arm while they took turns reading. Ryan hadn't shown. He hadn't called. And when they'd called his private number, all they'd gotten was voice mail.

"He didn't promise, sweetheart."

Kelsey had expected Ryan to be here in time to tuck his daughter in and frankly she was furious. She had to fight to keep the anger out of her voice. Almost choking on the oft-repeated words, she said, "He's a very busy man. I'm sure he wanted to be here. Something really, really important must have come up."

And if it hadn't, he was going to get hear about it from her.

"Could we read one more chapter?" The desperation in Mariah's voice was killing Kelsey.

"Only if you'll do the funny voices again."

Mariah managed a grin which only made Kelsey madder. If the man had any feelings at all he would be here. Didn't he understand how disappointed Mariah was to spend so little time with him? And he'd promised to be here tonight. Well, almost.

She wished she'd never mentioned Ryan's offer of coming to

snuggle time to Mariah. But he'd seemed so sincere, so approachable last night. She'd believed him.

Well, never again. She was a slow learner, but workaholic men like Ryan and Mark were too driven by their own egos to consider how others were affected by their neglect.

With more spirit than she felt, she launched into a new chapter of *Charlotte's Web*, providing the voice of Charlotte while Mariah oinked and neighed and quacked as the other animals in the barn. Anything to get her mind off the missing father.

Finally, the inevitable moment had come and she closed the book. Pulling the child into her arms, she hugged her as close as her tummy allowed. "Sorry, sweetness."

"It's okay," Mariah whispered against her shoulder.

But it wasn't okay and Kelsey didn't know what to do except offer herself in place of Ryan. "Do you mind if I lie here with you for a while?"

Mariah pulled back slightly. "Are you scared of the dark?"

"Just lonely sometimes."

"Okay. You can stay here. I'll keep you company." She snuggled closer. "Did you know your tummy moves a lot?"

Mariah bit back a laugh. "That's the baby moving around in there." She rolled to her back and placed Mariah's hand over her robe. "Feel that? I think that's a foot."

Mariah's eyes widened. "This is truly amazing. Does it hurt?"

"Not at all."

"I'm glad. I don't want anything to hurt you." Big chocolate eyes studied her for a few moments and then began to droop. "You're nice, Kelsey."

Kelsey kissed the smooth forehead. "Good night, sweetness."

Right before her eyes closed for the last time, Mariah murmured, "Daddy would have liked my pig voice."

And Kelsey thought her heart would break.

* * *

Three hours later, Kelsey sat in the living room, reading a book on postnatal care while waiting up for Ryan. He was not going to get away with ignoring his child any longer.

When the key sounded in the door, she braced for the coming battle. Fists tight at her side, back straight, she started through the kitchen to meet him. His back was turned away from her as he closed the door, but Kelsey couldn't wait another minute. She let him have it.

"How dare you disappoint your child this way! I can't believe how inconsiderate you are. All that money and no sense at all." She was just getting warmed up when he turned around. One look at him and all the wind went out of her.

Haggard and dirty and dejected, he stared at her through bloodshot eyes. His tie was gone. His shirt filthy and torn. Face smudged with gray and black, he smelled of smoke.

"Ryan?" She moved toward him, hand extended. "What is it? What's happened?"

He didn't answer. Rather he trudged like a man condemned into the den and collapsed, head in his hands.

Kelsey followed, despising the inopportune words she'd spoken when he was so upset. She stood in front of him, wringing her hands. "I'm sorry. Please. Can I get you something?"

He shook his head.

Kelsey could feel his need but was at a loss. Without a second thought, she knelt in front of him and placed a hand on each of his knees, hoping that human comfort would help whatever was wrong.

The baby moved inside her as if understanding her turmoil. The beat of her own heart and the ragged sound of Ryan's breathing were the only sounds. Finally, after she'd despaired of ever getting him to tell her, he began to speak.

In a rough, hoarse voice, he said, "There was a fire in one of my buildings."

The sirens? Were they on their way to Ryan's fire?

"Oh, my goodness! Your office building? Are you hurt?"

His dark head moved from side to side. "Not my office. Another of my buildings. One that was being renovated."

"What happened?"

"Don't know yet. It's still smoldering. Too soon for the investigators."

"Were there people inside?" She knew the answer before she asked. No one would be this upset over a building.

"Most got out. But not everyone. Three construction workers are in the burn unit now." He shuddered. "Have you ever seen a man being burned alive?"

The horror of his question sent her stomach topsy-turvy.

"No," she whispered. "I'm so sorry. It must have been a terrible thing to see."

"Unbelievable. The heat and smoke." He dropped his hands and stared at them. They were black with soot. "The screaming…"

All the time she'd been castigating him for not being present for Mariah's bedtime, he'd been watching helplessly as people burned in an inferno.

"What can I do?" she asked. "Let me do something, Ryan. I need to…"

Yet what could she do to erase the sounds and sights playing though his head?

He raised his face then, looking bleakly through red-rimmed eyes. And without a word, he reached out, pulled her toward him. Kelsey was so surprised she didn't think to resist. She just went into his arms and held him.

Strong, powerful Ryan Storm trembled with unspeakable

emotion. Face pressed into his shoulder, Kelsey smelled smoke so strong her stomach churned and she needed desperately to move away for fresh air. But she didn't. Ryan was a self-contained, self-possessed man, who normally needed no one. Tonight, he needed the comfort of another human being. He needed her.

All her ugly judgments concerning him gathered at the base of her brain. She'd considered him unfeeling, uncaring, self-focused. Was this the reaction of a man fitting that description?

There was a lot more humanity inside Ryan than she'd given him credit for.

As she leaned against him, trying to soak in his stress, her mind raced with a dozen questions about the tragedy. For once in her life, she kept her questions to herself. There would be time for all that later. Right now, her purpose was comfort. And she could do that.

Minutes ticked by while heavy oppression hung like a fog in the room. Gradually, Ryan relaxed but didn't loosen his hold. Instead, he leaned back into the arm of the sofa, pulling her with him. Arms around him, Kelsey lay with her head on his chest, over the thudding heart. Neither of them spoke. Kelsey because she didn't know what to say, while Ryan seemed lost in his troubled thoughts.

He held her for such a long time, with silence surrounding them, that Kelsey became aware of him in a new way. His back muscles where her fingers grazed in embrace were tight and smooth and hard. His belly was flat and taut where his torn shirt exposed dark skin and a thin line of hair above the waistband of his ruined slacks. The arms that clasped her to his side were amazingly strong and curved with flexed muscles. Ryan Storm might sit behind a desk, but his body was that of a workman.

She'd noticed before, but now, touching him, she noticed more than ever.

To her shame, she was actually turned on. Men were in the hospital suffering. Ryan was in despair. And she was thinking about his body.

She started to lever up and away from him, but with her center of gravity pulled forward, her movements proved awkward. Ryan moved with her, hands coming around her hips to steady her. Too late, she tumbled forward onto him. With a grunt of lost breath, he caught her and in one swift movement had them both on their feet. But instead of letting her go, he held on.

"It's late. You should get some sleep," he said, the smoky gruffness in his voice both sexy and disturbing.

She nodded. "So should you. You have to be exhausted."

"Yeah." He sighed, a big gusty sound of forced relaxation. Kelsey knew he'd sleep little tonight.

"Could I get you something to eat first? Some wine?"

"No." And this time he released her. "Go on."

She stood there, uncertain about leaving him alone, needing to make everything better and knowing she couldn't.

"Well, good night then."

Before she could turn away, he caught her elbow. "Kelsey," he murmured. And something in the sound jump-started her heart. He took one step, one infinitesimal step and bent his head. Kelsey's heart thundered erratically. She was no innocent child. Ryan wanted to kiss her. And she wanted him to. In the next second, he brushed his warm mouth across hers in a kiss of exquisite tenderness. Kelsey swayed, wishing for more, but Ryan released her just as suddenly as he'd begun.

With a look that left her confused and bewildered, he turned and left the room.

* * *

The next day, as the business world and media swirled around him like pesky gnats, Ryan couldn't get his mind off the nanny. He'd kissed her, for Pete's sake. He couldn't believe he'd done such a foolhardy thing.

Yes, he'd known from the start that she was no ordinary nanny, but he'd crossed the line. The woman was a widow of less than a year. He'd still been a basket case a year after Amanda's death.

Yet he'd wanted to hold on to Kelsey forever. Her sweetness, her kindness in being there for him last night, really got to him. He couldn't get past how much it had helped to hold her.

But the woman was an employee. A pregnant employee.

He shouldn't have hired her. That's all there was to it. A man running on Starbucks espresso, no sleep and high stress should not make decisions in crowded airports.

With a groan, Ryan tossed aside the pen in his hand and shoved back in the silky smooth-rolling chair. Last night had been a nightmare. And he still hadn't awakened.

His intercom buzzed. He pressed the button. "Yes."

"Mr. Storm, John called from the hospital. No change."

"Thanks, Marian." He'd expected no more. The doctors had said the first few days were the most critical.

"Those reporters are still out here."

"Give them the prepared statement and call Stan. Tell him to arrange a press conference."

"Will you be there?"

"Hell, no." He was no hero. Didn't they understand that? The heroes were in the hospital, fighting for their lives.

He spun toward the window, looking out over the sprawling Dallas-Fort Worth Metroplex. It was a blustery day, cloudy, gray and cold, but thankfully there was no snow. The fire marshal needed time to dissect the cause of the blaze that had destroyed a high-rise office building, critically wounded three of his construction workers and sent several firefighters to the hospital. From here, if he strained his eyes and used his imagination, he could make out the empty spot on the Dallas skyline.

His own office sat at the top of a skyscraper owned by Storm International. Throughout the building his companies, his investments, his employees functioned as well-oiled machines, productive, cutting-edge, ready to move on anything innovative that could make money. He knew every employee in this building by name and position. He demanded excellence in all things and he paid well for it. He also demanded the highest safety standards. So what had happened?

Restless, worried and unable to concentrate, Ryan pressed the intercom again. "Any word from the fire marshal?"

"Nothing yet, sir. Miss Mason phoned."

Miss Mason? Kelsey? "Why didn't you put her through? Is anything wrong at the house?"

"Nothing she mentioned. She said not to disturb you. She just wanted to know if you were all right." The secretary's voice held a note of curiosity which he was not about to satisfy. "Are you?"

"I'm fine." Nothing a month's sleep wouldn't cure. He glanced down at his reddened hands. They would heal. He only prayed the workmen were as lucky. "If she calls again, put her through."

The vision of Kelsey's face, right before he'd kissed her, swam in the forefront of his memory. His stomach tightened. All through the long, sleepless night, he'd held to that memory, her fresh, clean scent helping erase the awful stench of smoke.

She'd been there when he needed her, and he was grateful.

More than grateful. That was the problem. Perhaps he should fire her.

Stupid thought. Fire a woman because he desired her. The problem was his, not hers.

She'd comforted him. Nothing more. Nothing less.

He'd been the one who stepped over the line, taking advantage of his employer status. He despised businessmen who did that. Yet, he was guilty.

He'd been wrong.

And he'd make sure she understood that.

Kelsey had heard Ryan pacing downstairs half the night. Unable to sleep either, she'd heard his husky murmur as he telephoned the hospital several times. More than once, she'd started to go to him, but after the kiss she couldn't. She wanted to offer friendship, a listening ear, solace. She feared he'd think something else, which was crazy considering her pregnant state. But she couldn't take that chance.

At some point, she'd fallen into a fitful sleep filled with the smell of smoke and dreams of Ryan's mouth and body touching hers.

Just before daylight, she'd awakened, haggard and worried, to the quiet hum of the garage door as Ryan left the town house.

According to his secretary, he was working and busy. Work, not people, was Ryan's solace. Had she forgotten? And yet, last night, he'd sought human comfort.

The telephone jangled and, with a glance at Mariah who was happily creating a map of the United States from colored Play-Doh, she picked up the receiver.

A female voice asked, "Is this Janine?"

"Janine doesn't work here anymore."

"Thank God," the woman said with a laugh. "Who is this? Abilena? Lord, girl, your English has improved."

"This is Kelsey Mason. I'm Mariah's new tutor."

"Well, I'll say it again. Thank God. Mariah is odd enough without growing up under the tutelage of that woman. But that's not why I called. Is Ryan all right? I saw the news reports."

Kelsey hadn't considered news coverage, but of course anything involving Storm International and a big fire would make the local news.

"May I ask who's calling?"

"Michelle, Ryan's sister. My brother may not like it, but his family does worry about him. When I saw the news where he'd rushed into that building, I nearly had a heart attack."

Kelsey's heart skipped a beat. "What? Ryan went into a burning building?"

"Girl, don't you watch television? Never mind. Since you work for Ryan, I know the answer to that. All work and no play. I hope you won't let him do that to you." The words came fast and furious and a little disjointed. "But yes, my macho brother charged into a burning building like some superhero and pulled out one of the injured men. The news is all over the television."

Kelsey slid slowly into a chair, one hand cradling the phone, the other cradling her baby. Ryan had gone into a burning building. He'd risked his own life.

"Oh my goodness. Oh my goodness." No wonder he smelled like smoke.

"Are you all right?" the voice on the other end asked.

"Yes, yes, of course I'm fine." But her hands were shaking. "It's Ryan I'm worried about. Though as far as I could tell last night, he wasn't injured. He left for the office before daylight."

"Well, unless he was half-dead, he wouldn't tell anyone. It's his superhero mentality. Ryan Storm, the invincible."

Michelle's attitude went from worried to flip and edgy as if she resented her brother but felt an obligation to voice concern. The Storms were a confusing bunch.

Kelsey, on the other hand, reeled from the news that Ryan had put himself in harm's way to save a workman. What kind of man did that? Where were the firefighters?

"Maybe you should phone his office and talk to him yourself," Kelsey suggested. "I'm just the nanny."

The woman he kissed last night.

"I will, if his dragon of a secretary will put me through." A small pause and then, "What did you say your name is?"

"Kelsey Mason. Ryan hired me because he knew me in high school. I think I remember you, too. You were a year ahead of me."

The woman made a noise in the back of her throat and then chuckled. "Well, don't tell anyone. I lie about my age and swear to be Ryan's younger sister, not the older."

Kelsey smiled into the phone. "I was Kelsey Slater back then. You may not remember me."

"Kelsey? Let's see." The sound of tapping, as if she tapped her nails against the phone. "I think I do. How nice that Ryan hired someone from the past. He doesn't usually do that. Let the past be the past, he always says, as if he can change who he was by ignoring it."

Though uncertain of the woman's meaning, Kelsey detected a bitter note in the comment. Ryan had been a puzzle in high school and she'd known little about him other than his reputation for leading a group of misfits and rabble-rousers and his habit of sleeping through classes. She'd thought him terribly exciting and dangerously sexy.

The trouble was, she still did.

"I think he was desperate," she blurted.

Michelle laughed. "Even desperate, Ryan never makes a decision that isn't advantageous. He hired you for a good reason. You can count on that. He's smart, you know, like Mariah, though he never had the chances for education that she will have."

"Is that why he pushes her so hard?"

"Still doing that, is he? It burns me up, girl. Ryan and I have had more than one shouting match over my little niece. It's not normal, I've told him, but he wants her to have all the advantages he never had."

"There's nothing wrong with that."

"No. It's the methods that drive me crazy and make Mariah weird."

If the woman called Mariah weird one more time, Kelsey was going to hang up on her. "Mariah is a wonderful child."

At the sound of her name, Mariah looked up and smiled.

"Of course she is. She's my niece and she's wonderfully sweet, but let's face the truth, Ryan is smothering her. She acts more like a young adult than a kid."

Kelsey had to agree. "I'm trying to change that."

"Well, good for you, girl. You give me a holler if there is anything I can do to help." She laughed. "Or to otherwise get under my brother's skin."

Kelsey laughed, too. Somehow, she thought she might like to get better acquainted with Ryan's sister. "Why don't you drop by sometime? I'd love a visit and I'm sure Mariah would."

"I'll do that, girl. I don't see enough of my niece or my hardheaded brother. If he gives you any grief, let me know. I'll give it right back to him. You take care now."

The phone went dead and Kelsey stood staring at it for a few seconds, the wheels in her head turning. What an interesting woman.

Even more interesting was the news she'd shared. Ryan had gone into a burning building. Dear Lord. He could have been killed.

No wonder he'd clung to her so long last night. He'd faced death.

But even that didn't explain the kiss.

CHAPTER SIX

AFTER THE CONVERSATION with Michelle, Kelsey thought long and hard about a lot of things. One of them was about what she would say and how she would react to Ryan when he arrived home. Would he mention the kiss? Should they just ignore it and go on? Somehow she couldn't do that. As much as she didn't want to be attracted to him, she was. Theoretically, she should leave. Realistically, she could not lose this job. She had a baby coming and a mountain of bills to pay. All her phone calls to the insurance company and attorneys in Seattle had fallen on deaf ears. Nobody cared about the widow. They just wanted their money.

And while her father was sympathetic to her plight, he hadn't thrown out the welcome mat. With a new wife half his age, he didn't want reminders that he was about to become a grandfather.

The other thing on her mind was, of course, Mariah. Even Ryan's sister agreed that the child needed more childlike fun in her life. As restless as Kelsey was after discovering Ryan's part in the fire, she decided a shopping trip was in order.

"Come on, honey," Kelsey said, reaching around Mariah to close the math book. "Enough study for one day."

"But I still don't understand this."

"Another day, it will be easier." Like two years from now. Mariah's forte was in verbal skills and language. Math beyond a second grade level gave her fits. "Come on, let's do something fun."

Mariah's brown eyes lit up but just as quickly dimmed. "Like what?"

"Go shopping."

"For what?"

"Oh, lots of things. Watercolors, for one."

"Really?" There was both hope and hesitation in that single word. "Aren't they extremely messy?"

"That's part of the fun. Come on, doll, let's go shopping."

They returned a couple of hours later, tired but happy. Anyway, Kelsey was tired. Her feet had swollen—a first—from all the walking. But the effort was worth the result. She had been able to release some of the stress from last night's events, and Mariah, still in the dark about her father's close call, had been delighted by the excursion. She had chatted up the store clerks, startling one with her knowledge of the Paleolithic paintings found in the caves of Altamira, Spain. She'd further quizzed the woman about whether the paints used by the ancient peoples would have been oils and where on earth had they acquired them?

The bemused clerk vacillated between amazement and amusement. Kelsey had saved the woman by explaining her role as tutor. That, too, had turned into something more when Mariah made a slight correction. Kelsey was, as she put it, Mariah's "tutor-slash-nanny" although she was still holding out for Kelsey to take the position of mommy.

Considering the kiss she couldn't forget, Kelsey decided it was time to make a hasty exit.

Now they were home again, loaded down with all kinds of supplies to make learning fun and less of a drudge.

"No one ever let me do this before," Mariah said as Kelsey spread newspapers on the table and laid out the supplies. "Miss Janine didn't approve of messes or messy children."

"Miss Janine was a stuffed shirt." Either that or she didn't enjoy cleanup.

"That's what Aunt Michelle says. Is Daddy a stuffed shirt, too?"

Aunt Michelle must have said that, as well, but Kelsey wouldn't touch the comment with a ten-foot pole. She might have thought it before, but after last night, she wondered if Ryan was actually a deep and sensitive man who hid his feelings behind work.

The problem with that train of thought was that it only made Ryan more attractive. Over and over, she reminded herself that he was: number one, her employer. Number two, a workaholic, driven by success. She'd already suffered the effects of falling for a man like that.

To sidestep the question, Kelsey held up boxes of instant lemon and chocolate pudding. "Which shall we paint with? Sparkling tempura or this pudding?"

"You can paint with pudding?"

"Sure can." Kelsey tied a plastic trash bag around her waist.

"I think I'd rather eat it."

"We can do that, too, if you'd like."

"Pudding it is," the child exclaimed. "Oh, this is going to be delicious fun."

"A pun," Kelsey exclaimed, laughing as she set out the equipment and ingredients and explained the definition of a pun. "I couldn't have said it better."

Under her direction, Mariah measured and mixed the pudding, splattering bits of chocolate while making up a dozen more puns to share with her daddy. Ever-tidy Mariah wiped up every tiny spot and spatter, keeping the area sparkling clean. Michelle was right. The child needed to cut loose and have some messy fun.

And the distraction was exactly what Kelsey needed.

With the two colors in bowls between them and slick finger-paint paper laid out on the table before them, they began to paint. As Kelsey had expected, Mariah was wonderfully creative, carefully planning her picture to incorporate the brown and yellow to best advantage. In the run of conversation, Kelsey tossed out art concepts along with painters' names and styles.

Best of all, though, was the giggling and silliness. With every giggle, Mariah, out of habit, placed both hands over her mouth. And since both hands were covered in pudding, so was her face. The more she did it, the funnier it was until both Kelsey and Mariah were laughing so hard and having so much fun they didn't hear the garage door open.

"What is going on in here?"

Kelsey jumped, throwing her hands out in surprise, and splattered chocolate pudding on the wall. Mariah glanced up, her painted mouth a surprised O. "Daddy."

Sure enough, Ryan Storm stood in the kitchen entry looking far too much like his last name.

"Why is my daughter wearing a trash bag?"

Kelsey's heart did the jitterbug. As if they had a mind of their own, her eyes looked straight at his lips. Oh my, he had a wonderful mouth and a bottom lip that was far too sensual for a staid businessman.

"You're home," she squeaked. And for a man who had been through a fire and done without sleep last night, he looked incredible. "Are you okay?"

He looked way more than okay, and she fought back the urge to stare at his mouth some more. She couldn't, however, fight off the blush creeping up her neck. Any minute now, her cheeks would flame and the freckles would flash like brown traffic lights.

Ryan scowled at her. With a slant of his eyes, he indicated Mariah's ever-listening ears. Kelsey got the message. Don't talk about the fire in front of the child.

Instead he seemed focused on the messy kitchen. He stood with hands on hips, suit jacket pushed back on either side, staring around the room.

Okay, so the kitchen was a mess. Big whoopee.

"You didn't answer my question. Is this supposed to be educational?"

"Of course it is," she said, reaching for a paper towel. She refused to back down now that she'd decided the best way to educate a genius child. Hadn't he agreed that creativity was important?

"Mind sharing exactly how?"

"Not at all." Though she couldn't look at him without imagining the kiss and worrying about the fire, she forced herself to stand straight and tall and look him in the eye anyway. "Art stimulates the right side of the brain. Finger painting develops fine motor skills. Mixing and measuring provides hands-on math instruction." She ended with a tiny sniff. "Need I go on?"

She sounded like a prissy old lady.

A corner of Ryan's lips twitched, and Kelsey was right back to thinking about the kiss again. "Please don't."

"Daddy?" Mariah said quietly. Taking her art by the corners she lifted it in his direction. "Do you like my jungle scene?"

Ryan's face softened. "It's very nice."

It was also drip, drip, dripping onto the gleaming tile.

"I made it just for you." Her smile was a thing of beauty and innocence.

What could the guy do? He took the soggy paper by the corners. "Thank you, peanut."

"It's impressionistic. See?" she pointed to the blurry yellow flowers. "Monet. Right, Kelsey?"

Kelsey lifted an eyebrow at Ryan in an "I told you" look. "Exactly right. Now, why don't you run upstairs and have a bath. I'll clean up the mess."

"Are you going to be here when I come back?" Mariah said to her dad. "We have some important issues to discuss before snuggle time."

He touched the top of her head. "I'm home for the night. Now run on up. I can hardly recognize my peanut under all that chocolate."

"I'm a chocolate-covered peanut," the little girl exclaimed and then went giggling out of the kitchen.

"She was really enjoying herself," Kelsey said.

"I noticed." He was also noticing her, or so it seemed from the intensity of his dark gaze. Slouched against a column that divided the formal dining room from the kitchen, he stood with arms crossed, studying her.

What was going on behind those chocolate eyes?

Was he judging her teaching skills? Was he remembering the kiss? Or was he just tired and staring?

The unrelenting silence made her jittery. She grabbed the soggy newspaper and began crunching it into a ball. "We saved you some pudding."

"I can't imagine there would be any left." His droll comment brought a smile.

"Did you have dinner?"

He shrugged off the question, so she never knew for sure if he had or hadn't.

From the refrigerator, she handed him a parfait glass layered with chocolate and banana pudding and topped with whipped cream. He took it to the table.

"Join me," he said, voice grave. "We need to talk."

Okaaay. So she was in trouble. Was he going to fire her over something as insignificant as a messy kitchen?

First things first. "How are the injured men?"

"Holding their own."

"Good." Breathing a sigh of relief, she poured them both a cup of coffee. Her hands shook the tiniest bit. Ryan was making her nervous.

Darn him for kissing her. Darn her for liking it so much.

After relegating her trash-bag apron to the garbage can, she took a chair across from him.

"You didn't tell me you'd gone into that building," she said softly as she stirred sugar into her cup.

His shoulder hitched again. "No choice. I was there. The firefighters weren't."

She could have argued the fact, but didn't bother. This was the way Ryan's brain worked.

"Still, what you did was amazing. A lot of people would not have gone in there. You could have been hurt."

An infinitesimal flick of his eyes toward his hands caught her attention. She looked down at them, too. "Did you burn yourself?"

That tiny shrug again. "It's nothing."

She reached for the hand closest to her. For a second, he resisted but when she persisted he turned his palm up. Red and hot as a sunburn, several blisters formed across the palm.

"Did the doctor check these?"

"I said it's nothing." His nostrils flared. "Nothing compared to what my men went through."

"You did everything you could."

With a sigh, he pulled his hand away. "I know. But it wasn't enough. I couldn't get to them…the smoke." He shook his head as though doing so would chase away the memory. "Jamie was on fire when I reached him."

Kelsey's stomach lurched at the nauseating image. "Oh Ryan. That's horrible."

"The smell of burning flesh…"

She pushed away her dessert, all appetite gone.

Ryan noticed. "You don't need to hear this."

"But you need to talk about it."

"Talking won't fix the problem." Metal clinked against glass as he moved the spoon up and down in the parfait, but didn't eat. "I'm okay. Let's talk about something else."

Frankly, Kelsey was relieved to change the subject before her unpredictable stomach sent her running for the bathroom. She said the first thing that came to mind.

"You're different from the boy I remember in high school." Still puzzling, but way different.

His face brightened a little as if he might smile. "Is that a good thing or a bad thing?"

"Both, I think. You were so lazy back then. Being tardy, falling asleep in class. Now you seem so driven." If not for his gang of friends taking notes and covering for him, he probably wouldn't have passed.

The hint of amusement faded to a wry sadness. "I was never lazy, Kelsey. I was working then, too. At night."

He scooped a spoon of dessert into his mouth. Kelsey tried not to watch the subtle movement of his lips.

"You worked at night and went to school, as well?" When he nodded, she said in soft amazement. "I had no idea."

All through high school she and others had misjudged the brooding teenager. Amazing to think he worked while she slept comfortably in her parents' home and awakened rested and ready for school. No wonder he slept in class. The boy had been exhausted.

Ryan shrugged as if all teenagers kept such a schedule. "Things worked out."

She'd say they had, and yet he still drove himself relentlessly, to the point of rushing into burning buildings. The man cut himself no slack. No wonder he expected so much out of his child. He held even higher standards for himself.

They sat in silent companionship for a few minutes. Ryan finished off the simple dessert while Kelsey wondered what his boyhood had been like. The moment was pleasant and unusual, given how little time he spent in his own home.

Even when he pushed aside his glass, Kelsey wasn't ready to end the conversation. Ryan had always interested her. In high school, she'd found his dark aloofness dangerous and sexy. He'd been a puzzle every woman wanted to solve.

He still was.

After a sip of warm, sweet coffee, she broke the quiet. "Mariah expressed an interest in taking music lessons. What do you think?"

"Do it."

"She wants to play the dulcimer. Medieval style."

He laughed. "That's Mariah. Do you have any ideas for a teacher?"

"I've called around but I'll want to check references before a decision is made."

"Good. Let me know. I want the best for her."

Kelsey bit her tongue to keep from saying the obvious. The best thing for Mariah would be a father who spent more quality time with her.

"She's a fascinating child," she said instead. "When did you first realize how gifted she is?"

Ryan let his spoon clatter to the bottom of the now-empty glass. He knew the answer to Kelsey's question almost to the day.

"When she was about three. Until then, I actually considered that she might be handicapped. If you can believe that."

Kelsey's face registered surprise. Her coffee mug clunked onto the table. "You must be kidding."

"Seriously." Memories of those days swamped him. Some good. Most bad. Mariah had been a wonderful infant, quiet and calm, as if somehow understanding that her father was too distraught to deal with a fussy baby. If not for the responsibility of caring for Mariah, he wasn't sure how he could have survived those dark and terrible months of gut-eating guilt and grief. That tiny bundle of life had given focus to his world. So that when she didn't begin to behave in the normally expected manner, he'd been near panic.

"She seemed bright and happy and interested, but she made no attempt to talk. No babbles, no da-da, nothing. She wasn't interested in baby toys, but she would sit for hours looking at books and TV. I had her hearing tested, her vision, everything. Doctors said she was very intelligent and would talk when she was ready."

"And they apparently were right."

Thank God, they had been right. Up until then, he'd wallowed in the fear that his baby had been damaged during those hours Amanda had been alone and dying. Hours when he should have been with her.

"One day just after her third birthday, she was sitting on the floor of my office, flipping through one of my books the way she loved to do. Suddenly, she brought the book to me, pointed and said, 'I don't know this word.'" He shook his head at the sweet, startling memory. "I nearly fell out of my chair."

"She was reading?"

"All that time. Reading and obtaining an enormous vocabulary." He was still a little chagrined about that turn of events. "Had I realized, I would have been more discerning about the kind of books I kept laying around. As it was, she pointed to a word I preferred she never learn."

"She taught herself to read," Kelsey said in wonder. "Amazing. Incredible. What a fabulous mind."

"Downright scary, if you asked me. What does a man do with a six-year-old who's smarter than he is?"

Kelsey lifted a shoulder. "The same thing you would do with any six-year-old, I guess. Love her. Teach her the things she needs to know to be a good human being."

"I wish it was that easy."

It drove him crazy that he was never really quite sure what was best for Mariah. At work, he was the master. Sure. Confident. And almost always right. With Mariah, he floundered, searching for the very best, longing to give her everything and always wondering if someday she'd say he'd done it all wrong.

Raising a genius daughter without the aid of a mother was more difficult that anything he'd ever done. If only Amanda had lived…

With ruthless determination, he banished the useless train of thought. What was done was done. No matter how much it haunted him and affected his child.

Something of his switch in moods must have seeped across the table because Kelsey reached out and touched the back of his hand. Her skin was cool against his, a relief to the throbbing burns. He probably should have had the injuries looked at.

Earnestly, Kelsey said, "Stop being so hard on yourself—and Mariah, too. Just be here for her. That's what she needs most. You. Let her be a normal little girl."

"But she's not normal." Her genius was both a gift and a curse.

He'd already seen the curse in the way other children in kindergarten had treated her. But money talked. With enough of it, Mariah could thumb her nose at anyone who didn't accept her as she was. By building a financial empire around her, he could spare her so much. After costing her a mother, it was the least he could do.

"But she needs to be treated as a normal child, Ryan," Kelsey was saying. "Most people are ordinary. If she's going to function in a mostly average world, she needs to understand what that's like. Her gifts can make her special or they can make her odd. It's your choice."

Here they went again. Arguing over differences in philosophy.

"Didn't we have this conversation once before?"

"We'll likely have it again if I keep working for you. Which brings me to a subject we haven't talked much about." She shifted in her chair and then swallowed. Ryan braced himself for another unpleasant confrontation. "I'd like to continue working here after my baby comes."

Baby. Oh yes. A very unpleasant topic. Tension sprang up inside his chest like an evil jack-in-the-box. His gaze dropped to her middle. "What does your doctor say? Are you feeling all right? Any problems?"

Though they were normal concerns for an employer to raise, his obvious anxiety in asking them wasn't. Kelsey blinked at him, head to one side in contemplation before she answered.

"I'm doing very well. The baby is strong and healthy. No problems at all. Please don't worry. I can still provide excellent care for your daughter."

"Good. Good." He ran a hand across the back of his neck and looked at a painting on the far wall. Anywhere but at Kelsey's pregnant body. "You'll let me know if anything changes."

"Ryan, I'm past six months. The only thing that's going to change is the size of my belly." She patted the growing mound and smiled. "Women have babies all the time and still take care of their other children." She blushed. "Not that Mariah is my child. I mean…I didn't mean…"

He brought his gaze back to hers. Those charming freckles had appeared and he was tempted, so terribly tempted to touch them. "I know what you meant. Feel free to make a nursery out of the extra room."

"That's so nice of you, Ryan. Really." She beamed as if he'd given her a million-dollar bonus instead of offering a spare room that no one used. "But if it's too much trouble, I can put the crib in with me."

"No trouble at all. Whatever you want. Just don't be lifting or moving things on your own. I'll get someone in next week to clear out the room and help you with anything you need done."

"I don't know what to say. Again, this is so nice of you. Thank you."

His chest filled with a strange sense of accomplishment. If she didn't stop looking at him that way, he wasn't sure what he might do. She made him feel special, important, powerful—like a man who could move mountains. Most people considered him those things already, though he'd never believed any of it. With her, he did.

Yes, Kelsey Mason was a dangerous woman. Dangerously beguiling.

"You have pudding on your nose," he said, the words tumbling out before he could stop them. And then, to make matters worse, he leaned forward and rubbed a thumb sideways over the spot. He'd wanted to touch her freckles, to feel the smooth velvet of her clear skin. It was even better than he'd imagined. Heat and silk and velvet. So incredibly soft.

Her warm breath sighed against his fingertips. The memory of that same softness sighing against his mouth came rushing back.

And just that quickly, he regained his senses and pulled away, keeping his hands firmly to himself.

"I owe you an apology," he managed. This was the reason he'd wanted to talk to her. To apologize. To make her understand.

Her eyes sparkled. "For wiping pudding from my nose?"

He didn't see the humor. "For last night."

The blush deepened.

"You needed a friend. I'm glad I was there for you."

Yes, she'd been there for him, all right. He couldn't forget it. Yet he must.

As if he had no self-control whatsoever, his eyes dropped to her mouth. This was ridiculous. He was known for his steely self-discipline.

"The kiss was completely inappropriate." He pushed away from the table and stood, eager to escape before he lost the battle and kissed her again. At the rate he was going, he'd better hurry.

With a ruthless determination usually reserved for the boardroom, he rasped, "I want you to know I do not make a habit of fraternizing with an employee. It will not happen again. Now if you'll excuse me, I have some phone calls to make."

CHAPTER SEVEN

HAD HE HANDLED THAT correctly?

Probably not.

With a resounding snap, Ryan closed the door to his study.

Definitely not.

Usually, he was self-confident when dealing with employees. No second-guessing, no problems making himself clear. But Kelsey befuddled him in the most disturbing way.

The pregnancy distracted him. No denying that either. She claimed to be healthy, but they'd thought Amanda was healthy, too. They'd ignored the signs. Or maybe he'd ignored them.

The old familiar guilt seeped in like an unwanted guest. With a deep sigh of unalterable regret, he flipped open his laptop and sat down at the desk.

The cursor blinked its blind eye.

Mariah needed someone like Kelsey. Someone young and full of laughter. He realized as much, even though her idea of educating a gifted child differed from his. She was cute about it, spouting off educational objectives like a textbook. Mariah was happy. He could hear it in her voice, see it in the bouncy walk that always made his heart glad.

His daughter was his life. He'd like to spend more time with her, but he wanted to give her a future, too. Everything he did was for her.

At least he and Kelsey had talked. That was the important thing. He had apologized for crossing the line. Everything would be fine now. He could forget about the kiss, forget how soft and sweet she was, forget how much he enjoyed listening to the gentle drawl in her voice. And he could deal with the pregnancy issue. He wasn't sure how just yet, but he'd think of something.

Could he hire a nanny for the nanny?

The idea made him chuckle, though the sound was self-mocking.

Tonight, he'd sat across the table from her for so long, listening to her talk, admiring the curve of her eyelashes and enjoying every minute of being with her that he'd almost forgotten why he'd wanted to talk to her in the first place.

Face it, Storm. All you really wanted was to kiss her again. There was no discussion to be had. You wanted to be with her.

All right, so he did. He was human, though some would argue the point. He was a man with needs and feelings, though he tried hard to keep them buried in work. He was proud of that, too. A man with no self-control shouldn't be running a billion-dollar enterprise.

He could handle it. He could handle anything. He always had.

And if he chose to enjoy the company of his daughter's nanny; no harm, no foul, as long as he maintained that professional distance.

Satisfied that he'd resolved the issue, he checked his watch. It was nine o'clock in the morning in Tokyo. Time to do a little business.

Kelsey sat at the kitchen table staring at the empty doorway for another fifteen minutes. *Fraternizing?* Was that what he called it?

The term rang in her ears as if he'd slapped her.

The great and mighty Ryan Storm did not *fraternize* with employees?

Well, if that didn't put her in her place, nothing would. Which was all well and fine. She didn't want to fraternize with a man like Ryan Storm. She wanted to take care of her baby, pay her debts and get on with her life—without some success-driven male messing with her mind. Or her lips.

With a sniff, she scraped back from the table and took the dishes to the dishwasher.

Okay, she'd admit it. She was embarrassed. Not that Ryan had blamed her for the incident, but his apology made her feel about as attractive as a rock. A fat, pregnant rock.

She took a deep breath and tried to think outside her hormones. Maybe she was overreacting. After all, she *was* only an employee. Just because she'd been a good listener was no reason to get upset over a friendly little thank-you kiss and subsequent apology. Ryan was a man. Men were physical. End of subject. She would do her job and try not to be so oversensitive.

"Kelsey?" Mariah tripped into the kitchen just as Kelsey finished drying her freshly washed hands on a paper towel.

"You look all clean and shiny." She pulled the pajama-clad child against her for a hug. "Would you like a snack? Your pudding is in the fridge."

"Where's Daddy?"

"In his office, I think." Though her answer was a guess, most of Ryan's time at home was spent in the office. Either that, or lost in the computer or on the telephone. The man never stopped working. Sometimes she wondered if he conducted business in his sleep.

"Oh." Mariah climbed up to the bar and accepted the parfait glass from Kelsey. "I do hope he can wrap things up before snuggle time."

"He absolutely will," Kelsey said with determination. Ryan

would be there for snuggle time if she had to drag him up the stairs. "Would you like to play a geography game on the computer until then?"

"The one with clues and spies?"

"That's the one."

"Oh, I'd love that. Last time I caught the spy hiding in Red Rock Canyon." She licked the side of her spoon. "Do you believe in UFOs? I don't. If beings from another planet arrived on Earth, wouldn't the news be broadcast on CNN? Daddy says they are absolutely everywhere. CNN, I mean, not UFOs. Nothing escapes their attention."

Kelsey smiled at the flow of logic from her charge. Mariah's happy chitchat could lift her spirits faster than the speed of light.

"If both you and your dad think so, I must agree. You've given it far more thought than I have."

"True. I think about it a lot. Is there more pudding?"

"Sorry sweetness. Has your dinner worn off?" At the child's nod, she went on. "Some popcorn perhaps?"

"I suppose, though pudding would be so much nicer. That was really fun, Kelsey, painting with pudding. I think Daddy approved, don't you? He smiled at my painting and said it was good."

"He loved it."

"I know. He loves anything I do. He's my daddy." She hopped off the bar stool. "I think I'll go up to the playroom now and start the game. Is that okay with you?"

"Fine. I'll be in as soon as I have my own shower."

Mariah contemplated Kelsey with great seriousness. "You have pudding on your nose."

"Still?" Kelsey's hand went to her face. The memory of Ryan's touch came flooding back but she brushed it away. Some things were better left alone.

* * *

An hour later, Ryan opened his office to Kelsey's knock.

Fresh and glowing in a shirt the color of fresh peaches, she looked as though someone had forced her to his door. He regretted her discomfort. It was his fault, after all. He'd been the one to cross the line.

"Need something?"

"Mariah was hoping you'd come upstairs for snuggle time."

He checked his watch. "Is it already that time?"

"Yes." The word was an accusation, though he wasn't sure why.

"I wouldn't miss it."

She offered a doubtful glance that had him wondering and then led the way up the stairs. From the back, he couldn't tell she was pregnant. Considering the conversation they'd had a short while ago and his vow not to fraternize with the nanny, he tried not to notice the pleasant sway of her behind and the shapely legs. He tried but failed. He was one of those men who thought pregnant women were beautiful. Beautiful and scary. He simply could not help admiring her.

And if her soft honeysuckle scent wafted back to him, what could he do? A man had to breathe.

"Daddy!" Mariah exulted when he entered her room. "Come on. You are going to have the time of your life." She patted the side of the little twin bed. "You lay down on this side and Kelsey on the other."

He and Kelsey lying down on the same bed? Uh-oh. "There isn't room."

"There's always room for the people you love," she said, her Pollyanna smile bright and charming. "Come on now, don't be shy."

A mocking voice in his head, he gave up and settled into the designated spot. Kelsey didn't seem quite as willing. He understood her reaction all too well.

"Why don't you two do this without me?" she said.

Mariah looked crestfallen. "Kelseeey. I've been anticipating this moment for days."

Kelsey touched her round tummy. "I don't think I'll fit. Sorry, sweetness. Why don't I sit in a chair beside you?"

Ryan knew he should be glad. He wasn't. The evil imp inside his head flashed visions of lying close to Kelsey, her mahogany hair brushing his skin, her sweet scent surrounding him like a cloud. Given their earlier conversation, he tried to banish the image.

"But we can't snuggle if you're in a chair." Mariah's bottom lip trembled. For whatever reason, this bedtime event was really important to his child.

"Surely, three great minds can come up with a sensible solution," he said.

Suddenly, Mariah brightened. "I have the best idea ever. Let's adjourn to your bed, Daddy. It's humonstrous ginormous." She giggled. "I made that up."

Ryan laughed, though the evil imp was shooting video inside his head again.

But his innocent child couldn't know that. She simply wanted time with her two favorite adults.

Wondering what Kelsey was thinking in all this, he glanced from Mariah to her. She looked away. A sprig of anxiety sprouted inside him. Was she upset? Had his bungling attempt to apologize hurt her feelings? Maybe he should raise her pay.

"Come on, Kelsey," Mariah begged. "Please."

Kelsey gnawed her bottom lip, looked at Mariah's expectant face and lost the battle.

"The ginormous bed it is," she said in a resigned voice.

Oddly light-hearted and a tad bit victorious for some weird

reason, Ryan pushed off the narrow twin bed and lifted a giggling, wiggling Mariah into his arms. He was glad for his child. That was all. His pleasure had nothing at all to do with spending time with the enchanting nanny.

The picture of reluctance, Kelsey gathered several books and followed them down the hall.

As soon as Ryan bounced Mariah onto his king-size bed, he recognized his mistake. His bed was huge and luxurious and terribly, terribly lonely.

What had he been thinking? First, he'd kissed the nanny and now he'd all but insisted she share his bed. Even though snuggle time was innocent fun, there was something frighteningly intimate about having a beautiful woman in his bedroom.

But this was for Mariah, he reminded himself again. He could endure a few minutes of personal torment for her sake.

Mariah insisted on sliding beneath the sheets, but Ryan was careful not to. He stretched beside his daughter atop the covers, fully dressed, propping a pillow behind his head. He noticed Kelsey did the same, though she was dressed in a robe while he still wore the day's shirt and slacks. Both of them were bare-footed, an added intimacy.

"We really must do this more often." Oblivious to the under-current in the room, Mariah opened one of the several books Kelsey had brought in. Knowing his daughter, she was reading all of them at the same time. "Daddy, we're currently reading *Narnia*. I don't know why I haven't read it before. I'm really enjoying it. The symbolism is fascinating. You read the part of Aslan. He's the hero, you know."

She looked at him with adoration and Ryan melted. Her happiness was worth everything, even the discomfort of being a little too close to the kissable nanny.

"And I'm the evil white witch," Kelsey said with a fake cackle of glee, though Ryan noticed she looked at Mariah and not at him.

Yes, he'd definitely give her a raise. Or a nice, fat bonus.

"And I read the rest," Mariah said, almost bursting with joy as she slithered down between the two adults.

Yes, he could do this. For Mariah.

The second thoughts began when Ryan was forced to move very close to Mariah to see the book. Kelsey had to do the same. As a result, they were hardly a whisper apart. He could see the yellow flecks in Kelsey's blue-green eyes, smell the flowers of her shampoo, feel the softness of her hair when it brushed across his skin.

His fertile imagination went crazy again, the evil imp flashing all kinds of images through his brain. That's what happened when an employer stepped over the line.

Still, he was having a good time. He worked extra hard to make his character realistic, using his deepest, most sophisticated voice for the royal Aslan. The sheer silliness of it brought chuckles of delight from his listeners. He was trying to impress his daughter, not the nanny. At least, that's what he told himself.

The others, in turn, outdid themselves. Kelsey was evil personified. Mariah's small voice alternately squeaked and deepened. Before long, Ryan threw propriety out the window to make them laugh. He was as silly, pompous or outraged as the plot required, adding sound effects for emphasis. Horses hooves, thunder, a lion's roar.

Mariah loved it. Her sweet giggle turned him to mush. And every time Kelsey read her part, Mariah watched her with an expression that brought a lump to Ryan's throat. Her need for a motherly influence was never more apparent.

Never mind that he couldn't get that kiss out of his head.

Never mind that he thought of Kelsey more than was appropriate considering the fact that she was both an employee and a pregnant widow. His inner demons were his own, and he could handle them. Kelsey was good for his child and for now, Mariah's needs had to come first.

At that moment, Kelsey laughed and the sound washed over him as warm and welcome as spring sunshine. Mariah's giggle joined in, her small hands pressed to her face, charming him. Pleasure built up inside Ryan's chest until he laughed, too.

As crazy as it sounded, he hadn't enjoyed anything as much as snuggle time in months. Maybe longer. He'd been working so hard for so long, he'd forgotten how to relax.

There was a time before Janine and the expansion of Storm International that he'd read to Mariah every day.

Why had he ever stopped?

CHAPTER EIGHT

"DO YOU THINK DADDY WILL BE here again tonight?" Mariah asked.

She was setting the table in the breakfast nook, careful to place each item in the correct spot while Kelsey stood at the bar slicing vegetables for a salad. Though the formal dining room was elegant and beautiful, the nook had become a kind of comfort zone where Mariah and Kelsey took their meals. This particular day, Abilena had left early for a doctor's appointment, leaving a pork loin with apples and sweet potatoes in the oven. Kelsey and Mariah were happy to do the rest.

"He hasn't missed the last two nights," Kelsey answered.

She was still shocked by that turn of events. Though he often arrived at the last minute to toss his jacket on a chair, kick off his shoes and collapse dramatically next to a delirious and giggling Mariah, Ryan nonetheless arrived in time for snuggle-time.

Kelsey didn't know if she was happy about that or not. Last night, she'd managed to beg off the nightly reading, claiming Ryan and Mariah needed some quality time alone. But the truth was something else. Snuggling next to Mariah, listening to the deep rumble of Ryan's voice, trading amused glances over the top of Mariah's head caused her imagination to go wild. What if this was her child, her house, her man?

Those were not good thoughts. Not now, not ever. After the disaster with Mark, she had better sense.

"I do hope he can be here tonight," Mariah went on. "I tried calling him earlier. I wanted his opinion about what book to read next, but he was in a meeting. We're nearly finished with Narnia, you know. Do I have to write a report about it?"

Kelsey looked at her charge in surprise. Mariah seldom wanted to "bother" her father at work. "No written report."

Mariah poured milk into her glass and sat down. "See? That's why you're the best tutor ever. Janine was a dear lady. Really she was, but she didn't know the definition of fun. Ever since you told Daddy and me about the importance of play and socialization skills in children, I've been studying the topic. You're right, you know. And I'm trying my very best to be more normal."

The little speech was delivered as regular conversation but Kelsey saw beneath the words to the meaning. She stepped behind Mariah's chair and hugged her. "You are wonderful the way you are, Mariah. Don't ever change. All I want is for you to be happy and to make the most of your marvelous gifts."

"I know. That's why I love you."

Kelsey's heart squeezed. "I love you, too."

"Well, that's settled. Now can we eat?" Mariah shook out her perfectly folded monogrammed napkin and placed it neatly in her lap.

With a chuckle, Kelsey sat down and began dishing up the meal.

Before she could take the first bite, a male voice said, "I hope you saved enough for a hungry man."

Kelsey's stomach dipped. Ryan.

With an excited squeal, Mariah hopped out of her chair and threw her arms around him. "Daddy. You're here."

"And starving. No time for lunch today."

An astonished Kelsey couldn't remember ever taking a meal,

other than breakfast, with Ryan. While Mariah flitted around like a happy butterfly, Kelsey pushed out of her chair to get another place setting, all the while battling down her own feelings of pleasure. What was it about him that could turn a mundane meal into an event?

"If we'd known you were coming," she said, "we would have eaten in the formal dining room."

"No need. This is great. I like it better myself." He stripped off his tie and jacket. Even after a long day, he looked Wall Street wonderful. "You two go ahead. I'll wash up and be right back."

"We'll wait, won't we, Kelsey?" Mariah asked.

"Absolutely," she said for Mariah's sake, though considering her foolish reaction to his sudden appearance, she would be better off eating somewhere else. "This is a red-letter day."

Kelsey then had to explain the meaning of "red-letter day" to the ever-curious Mariah.

Ryan returned, sleeves rolled back, well-toned arm muscles too visible for comfort, to sit next to Mariah and across from Kelsey at the small round table. Why couldn't the man be wimpy and weak and a little less handsome?

He rubbed his hands together before shaking out a napkin. "This looks amazing. Abilena has outdone herself."

"Kelsey and I made the salad and bread."

"Really?" Ryan's gaze found hers and held steady. "Kelsey makes bread?"

"I love to make bread," Kelsey said, not adding that bread baking was a kind of therapy for whenever she was stressed. And how could she deny the stress? Yesterday, she'd received a final notice from a collection agency. Today they'd called, demanding payment in full. Somehow she'd convinced them to accept small monthly payments until Mark's insurance settled. If that ever happened. "But Mariah helped. She also created a fabulous dessert."

"Dirt cake. With *worms,*" Mariah's expression of disgust was all for show. She was really impressed with the dessert. "Daddy, it's so gross, you will love it."

Ryan chuckled. "Dirt cake with worms. Sounds interesting." He glanced at Kelsey again. "Studying decomposers, I suppose?"

"Actually no. We were having fun." Every thing she did with Mariah educated, but sometimes she liked getting under Ryan's skin the way he got under hers.

Mariah knew her daddy too well. She said, "Fun with fractions. Kelsey has really helped me with my math. Fractions make sense when you use measuring cups and spoons."

A forkful of golden yams halfway to his mouth, Ryan's dark, dark gaze settled on Kelsey. "Not a bad idea. What else is going on in the schoolroom?"

Ah, the schoolroom. She swallowed a bite of juicy, sweet apple and said, "I've been wanting to talk to you about that."

"Why do I get the feeling I might not like this?" He slid the yams into his mouth and chewed in speculation.

"You will. It's only paint and a few decorations." When he arched an eyebrow, she went on. "The room is so boring I nearly fall asleep in there. I've rearranged some things—"

He dropped his fork. "You've what?"

"Rearranged. We moved some tables into the room, set up a computer center—"

Before she could go on, he held up a hand. "Didn't I tell you not to be lifting anything? I can get someone to do that for you."

"No need. It's done."

"Don't do it again." He was serious. The man barked orders as though he was king.

Kelsey wanted to argue, but she wanted to redecorate that awful school room even more. She bit back her angry reply and said instead, "I'd like to paint a mural on one wall."

"Can you paint?"

She offered him a look that she'd be stupid to attempt a mural if she couldn't paint, but she only said, "Some. I also use patterns and stencils."

His gaze dropped to her round belly. "Aren't paint fumes harmful? I mean, to the baby?"

"Not the kind I'd use. Did you know there is substantial research about how important the right color and lighting is to learning and health?"

"You're starting to sound like Mariah. How do you know all this?" His gaze was quizzical and amused as he forked another bite of pork.

"I'm a teacher. It's my job to know." Besides, she liked tossing out these little tidbits to prove her points about Mariah's education. Taking up a knife, she sliced off a tiny portion of roast.

"Do whatever you think best as long as I see results. Take the credit card. Get what you need."

Now it was her turn to be surprised. "You trust me with your credit card?"

His mouth twitched. "Are you planning to run off to Tahiti on it?"

She laughed. "I'm not running anywhere with this baby around my middle."

Although a less-honest person might take his credit card and pay some overdue bills. Come to think about it, a less-than-honest person wouldn't worry about those debts in the first place.

A funny look crossed Ryan's face and, falling silent, he concentrated on his food. Every time the topic of her pregnancy came up, he grew tense and silent this way. Was he simply uncomfortable with the idea of pregnancy in general? Or was something else going on in that head of his?

She let the subject drop, content to know she and Mariah could now create a much healthier, more intellectually stimulating learning environment. And the room would be more fun, too.

"Daddy," Mariah said. "I do hope you can find time to come to our play. It's going to be a raving success and ever so much fun. Educational, too."

"A play?" He glanced from Mariah to Kelsey and back. "When is this happening?"

Kelsey let Mariah tell the story. The child was beside herself with excitement over the whole concept.

"Oh, we haven't set a date yet. The performance itself is still in the planning stages. We've almost completed the script, though. The story is magnificent, even if I do say so myself."

"You're writing a play? By yourself?"

"Yes, and Kelsey's teaching me to keyboard so we can put all the information on the computer. And I'm designing and printing all the invitations."

He got that bewildered look that said his daughter's intellect scared him spitless. "What's this play about?"

"Metamorphosis. Isn't that the loveliest word? Metamorphosis." She savored the term as she would a bite of ice cream.

"Indeed it is. And keyboarding, too. Impressive." He looked up at her, and Kelsey saw that the reserve had slipped away again. Once past that barrier, Ryan was pleasant company. Very pleasant.

"Mariah's story is about a homely little caterpillar who dreams of being popular."

"Kelsey, don't tell him! I want him to watch the play."

"Oh, sorry." She widened her eyes at Ryan who grinned in response. He really had the most engaging grin. The kind that made women wonder what he was thinking—about them.

"You'll have to come to the performance to hear and see the full story."

"We're inviting everyone we know," Mariah exclaimed.

When Ryan lifted a questioning brow, Kelsey reassured, "Not exactly everyone. We've asked the two neighbor kids to participate, since the play has three characters."

"And we're sending invitations to a few select individuals," Mariah said. "Special people." She winked at her dad and whispered conspiratorially, "Be looking for yours."

He tapped the end of her nose. "Will do, peanut, but my schedule is pretty tight right now."

Mariah's happy face fell. Averting her eyes, she twisted the napkin in her lap. After a momentary struggle, she said, "That's all right. I understand. You're quite busy right now with the Toliver takeover and all. I was just hoping…"

Even with her heart breaking, the child tried to please her daddy by hiding her disappointment. The idea that he couldn't take off from work long enough to do this one thing for his child made Kelsey so mad, she wanted to scream.

How could he do this? How could he be warm and wonderful one minute and an oblivious jerk the next?

"Really, Ryan, it wouldn't take that much of your time. It's a one-act play, for goodness sake. And we can present it on a Saturday. Even though you hole-up inside that office of yours most weekends doing lord only knows what, you can come out long enough to watch a one-act play that your own daughter created."

Ryan chewed his bite of pork, all the while watching her as if she'd grown another head. When she finally stopped talking, he swallowed, took a sip of tea and asked in a voice as cool as the ice floating in his glass, "Are you finished?"

Finished? She'd only begun. But getting into an argument

with Ryan wouldn't help Mariah. She stifled the rest by saying in her most sincere voice, "Please try to be here."

He set his tea glass aside and studied the slow roll of condensation sliding down the sides. Whatever was going on in his brain took some consideration.

Kelsey's stomach fluttered. Had she pushed him too far? During the last few evenings of snuggle time, she'd been sure he was becoming more aware of his daughter's need to see him every day. Had she ruined everything by saying too much too soon?

"Make it two weeks from this coming Saturday," he said. "And I'll be there."

Mariah's eyes widened. "Really? You really will?"

Ryan made an X on his chest. "Cross my heart. Now, where's this nasty, disgusting, wormy cake you promised."

While Mariah and Ryan teased one another about the dirt cake, Kelsey leaned back in her chair, relieved, both for herself and her charge. Ryan wasn't upset by her tirade. Maybe all the man needed was someone to shake him out of his work-induced haze now and then. Three nights ago and again today, he'd recognized Mariah's need and responded.

Beneath the workaholic suit was a pretty decent guy. A guy she already liked more and more every day.

She crammed a potato into her mouth with a stern reminder. Ryan Storm did not fraternize with employees. Thank goodness.

The afternoon of the play dawned cool and rainy, but nothing could dampen spirits at the Storm house. The place buzzed with anticipation and excitement as Ryan entered the living room.

He had nearly killed himself and his assistant all week clearing the decks enough so that he could attend. His neck ached from hours last night at the computer. And he was tired to the bone.

But he was here and if he'd admit it, glad to be.

One look around the overstuffed living room and he thought everyone else was here, too. Mariah had invited her Aunt Michelle, Abilena, her husband Julian who took care of the yard, their grandson Tito, a couple of kids Ryan didn't recognize and the two Clonts children from down the street along with their mother.

With Kelsey's help and direction, his daughter had transformed the living room into a mini-theater with seating for the guests along one wall. A series of mismatched curtains, probably dug from storage, were strung across one corner for the stage. He had no idea what was behind those curtains.

Having just come out of his office, Ryan moved around the room, greeting the visitors and doing his part to make everyone feel welcome. He had a million things to do, but he'd turned off his cell phone and would leave it off for the next couple of hours to concentrate solely on Mariah's performance. Otherwise, Kelsey would have his head.

He smiled. Tammy Clonts smiled back, taking the action as meant for her. In truth, he was thinking about Kelsey. She was a fireball, taking him to task over Mariah like a she-bear over her cub. She'd been right, too.

His pushy nanny had opened his eyes to a lot of things lately, one of those being his daughter's needs, both educational and emotional. The other wasn't so good. She'd made him realize how empty his own life was. Maybe he needed a vacation, something he'd never even considered before.

Right now, he couldn't spare the time.

"My kids have had such fun being involved with Mariah's play," his blond neighbor was saying. "Thank you for letting them participate."

"I'm afraid I can't take credit. Kelsey's the mastermind behind today. And Mariah, of course," he hastened to add.

Where were they anyway? He glanced around and caught a glimpse of Kelsey in the hallway making last-minute adjustments to the children's costumes.

Neither had mentioned the unfortunate kiss again. If he'd offended her, she covered it well. He'd managed to keep a professional distance, and even though he insisted she be present at snuggle time, that was his prerogative as her employer, nothing personal there at all.

Snuggle time. Another of Kelsey's magical additions to his household and one that he'd come to enjoy. So much so that he tried to arrive in time for dinner, as well. A man had to eat. Might as well eat with his daughter. And if his attention was sometimes too focused on Kelsey, well, she was an adult. A man needed adult conversation, too.

"I like your new nanny, little brother."

He whipped around to find his sister watching him watch Kelsey. Great. Now she'd be reading something into it.

"I was checking to see if they were ready to start." His was a lame excuse and he knew it.

She gave him a speculative smile but kept her thoughts to herself. For which he was grateful. Michelle had a habit of pushing her nose into his business. She'd even had the audacity to tell him to get over Amanda and move on with his life. As if that was possible.

"The players are sneaking into the back of the stage," she said. "Better grab a seat."

The dining-room chairs had been commandeered for seating, so he settled into one of them as Kelsey stepped in front of the makeshift stage. She was dressed in what she called a tunic and leggings. The top was a shade of green that turned her eyes to sparkling aquamarines.

"Ladies and gentlemen, if I may have your attention, please."

The room quieted.

"Thank you so much for coming to our play. Mariah, Tristan and Chelsea have worked very hard for several weeks to put this together. We have to thank Tammy Clonts for helping make costumes, Abilena Rueda for providing our refreshments and of course, Ryan Storm for so graciously allowing us to turn his living room into a theater."

She smiled in his direction and Ryan felt as if he'd actually done something worthwhile. He could feel his sister's eyes boring holes in the side of his face. He kept his focus on the curtain which wiggled and moved in tandem with a chorus of loud whispers and nervous giggles.

"Now, if everyone is ready," Kelsey went on. "Please enjoy the original play by Mariah Storm, 'Metamorphosis.'"

Dramatically, she thrust one hand toward the curtain which slowly parted.

Everyone clapped, the adults exchanging indulgent looks, and the play commenced.

Kelsey tiptoed to the open seat between him and Michelle and sat down. Her arm brushed his, and Ryan's nerve endings came to vivid life. He didn't consider it strange that he was so aware of her every move. After all, he needed to keep an eye on her health. What was strange was the tingling sensation that ran through him with every incidental touch.

He heard Mariah's voice then and, with the iron will that made him a good businessman, turned his attention to the stage.

The play was short and endearingly sweet, a tale of an ugly caterpillar who suffered from the harassment of others because of her lack of beauty. Mariah played the caterpillar with an aching poignancy that had him wondering. Did she feel like a misfit among her peers? Probably. And the notion cut him through the heart.

In the last lovely scene, Mariah shed the dull gray, oversized paper chrysalis that covered all but her soft dark eyes and fluttered forth in glittered, gossamer wings made from plastic wrap and cardboard. He'd known this part was coming but Mariah's sudden change from outcast caterpillar to beautiful butterfly brought a surprising lump to his throat.

A true metamorphosis was taking place in his daughter, and he'd be a fool not to acknowledge the woman at his side as the reason. Impulsively, he reached for Kelsey's hand and squeezed. When she glanced his way, eyes alight with pride at Mariah's success, Ryan pulled her hand onto his lap and kept it there.

The play ended and the children rushed behind the curtain only to return for a bow when the audience applauded. For Ryan, the moment was priceless, and he was glad Kelsey had remembered to set up the video camera. This was a film they'd watch over and over together, he was certain, but nothing had been better than being here. He was glad Kelsey had insisted. He supposed he should tell her as much.

Kelsey stood to thank the audience and to remind them again of the refreshments waiting in the dining room. As her fingers slid away from his, Ryan resisted the urge to stand with her, hand in hand. Michelle would give him enough grief over Kelsey as it was.

He let her go and then stood, seeking out his daughter. Unfortunately, she was with Kelsey, beaming for all she was worth as the visitors gathered around to offer congratulations.

That was the trouble with him and Kelsey. He couldn't seem to find the right balance. As her employer he needed to remain professional and aloof. As a man—well, he needed to forget that part. He was her employer and that was that.

CHAPTER NINE

IN THE WEEKS FOLLOWING the play, winter began to lose its grip and Kelsey's baby seemed to grow exponentially. According to her doctor, all was well and the baby would arrive on time, though she had yet to save enough money for many baby items, including the crib. Ryan had long since hired someone to clear out the spare room so it sat ready but mostly empty.

Each day she watched the classifieds hoping for a bargain.

This afternoon, the sun had come out and the temperature crept up into the fifties. For good-weather days, Kelsey tried to have an outing of some sort planned for her charge, and today appeared to be one of those.

She laid aside the infant blanket she had been cross-stitching. She was teaching Mariah to cross-stitch, too, but at the moment, Mariah was practicing the dulcimer with her usual concentration, the stringed melody *thwanging* gently.

Mariah's playgroup was coming along nicely, too, even though there had been a few incidents where Mariah's feelings had been hurt by children who thought she was showing off her intellect. After the success of the play, Kelsey believed more than ever that this kind of give-and-take was good for Mariah as long as her self-esteem was preserved. The play had done wonders for her in that respect, and she'd formed a friendship with the children who'd been here that day. Though Mariah preferred the company of adults, her comfort with other children was improving.

Janine's idea of an educational plan had long ago gone by the wayside. And if Ryan frowned and grumbled and raised his eyebrows, at least he didn't make her stop. She and Mariah blew soap bubbles, played dollies, did project after project with Play-Doh and art and went to the zoo to research the major animal groups. The school room was now a child's wonderland of learning, filled with stimulation and beauty.

Abilena graciously encouraged the daily invasion of her kitchen for creative endeavors and an hour or so of Spanish instruction for both Kelsey and Mariah. As a result, lunch had become a daily experience resulting in foods such as ants-on-a-log, lizard skins and candle salad. True to her nature, Mariah always saved some of her creations for Daddy which he ate with much fanfare and a sparkle in his eyes. Mariah was beside herself with happiness. Kelsey had to admit she appreciated his enthusiasm.

Ryan had changed since the play. He was home more, especially in the evenings. Even on the nights when he was sequestered in his office, he never missed snuggle time. Most evenings, he found time to play a game of chess or backgammon or even something silly such as charades. Kelsey found herself drawn into the activities as though she was part of the family. The notion both hurt and pleased.

Even though Ryan still questioned the educational value of some of her methods, he didn't stop them. The fact became an ongoing, though friendly debate that gave way to a running joke. He called her a flake. She called him stuffy. Mariah, once certain the adults were not really angry, found this hilarious.

For good or for bad, Kelsey's opinion of Ryan Storm was

slowly changing. He was still a workaholic, but at least he was aware now and trying. And if he smiled too easily at Kelsey, she refused to remember that one moment when he'd let down his guard and kissed her. He'd made it clear in a dozen ways since that the kiss had been an aberration brought on by stress and exhaustion.

The trouble was, she told herself, she'd been too long without any real male attention. Her marriage had been dead long before Mark was. Ryan was a complex man, smart and witty and compassionate, though he blew off any comments of praise. Any woman would find him attractive. Maddening at times, but also intriguing.

Add to this, Mariah's occasional reminders that she was still lobbying for a mother, and Kelsey had to fight not to feel too domestic. It would be easy to pretend that this was her home, her child, her man.

Every time the thought came, she laughed at her foolish fantasy. She was pregnant, in debt up to her eyebrows, and Ryan barely approved of her as a teacher. He would never be interested in someone like her. Hadn't he made that clear over a glass of chocolate pudding?

This was all well and good, as far as Kelsey was concerned anyway. No matter how much he had changed for Mariah, Ryan was still too success-oriented, too driven and too much like Mark in that respect. She wouldn't be hurt that way again.

She pushed out of the chair, glad she'd gained only the required amount of weight so far and was still agile and active. She and Mariah had been riding bikes every day for exercise and fun. Today would be even better.

"Want to try out your new roller skates? The weather looks good."

They'd shopped yesterday for the pink helmet and knee pads

to go with a fabulous pair of skates for Mariah. Kelsey hadn't skated in a while, but her in-lines were in the boxes she'd had shipped from Seattle.

Mariah carefully placed the dulcimer in its case. "May we go now? I've been positively phosphorescent with excitement."

Kelsey stifled the laugh. "Well, you *are* glowing, I'll have to admit." She clapped her hands. "Come on, little firefly, let's rock and roll!"

Mariah hopped to her feet.

"Roll being the operative word?" she asked with a happy grin.

"That's the idea," Kelsey said. "You're going to love it."

In minutes they were outfitted and outside, a cool breeze ruffling their hair, the sunshine invigorating. Kelsey loved to in-line skate, loved being outside and, after spending so much time indoors, her body needed the exercise and fresh air.

Mariah held tightly to the railing along the front walkway but her attention was on the complex of sidewalks in the gated neighborhood leading to a small central duck pond.

"May we skate to the pond and feed the ducks?" she asked. "We could take bread crumbs and pretzels and identify the various species."

Kelsey shook her head. "Maybe next time. Today we teach you the fine art of standing up. Once that's accomplished we can venture farther from the house."

The little girl looked disappointment but didn't argue. Kelsey, who had not been on skates during her pregnancy, was surprised at her own awkwardness. There was no way she'd chance either of them taking a hard fall.

Mariah wobbled along, arms out for balance. Occasionally she slid to the ground, unhurt, and bounced right up, laughing. "This is fun."

"Precisely."

After a few minutes of getting their legs under them, Kelsey held Mariah's hand and slowly, slowly led her down the sidewalk. They waved at neighbors coming and going, at a gardener preparing the soil for early planting, at Tammy Clonts getting her into her SUV. Mariah was so proud of her latest accomplishment, Kelsey thought she just might be as phosphorescent as she'd stated.

When a familiar metallic blue BMW rolled into view, Kelsey experienced the usual disturbing buzz of energy. As much as she tried to believe that the feeling was excitement for Mariah's sake, she knew she was only lying to herself. Seeing Ryan every day had become a much-anticipated moment for her as well as the child.

Yes, she was an idiot of the first order.

Mariah lifted a pink-nailed hand and waved at her father, her smile wide and thrilled. They'd played beauty shop before lunch and polished each other's nails.

"Daddy will be so proud of me. Maybe we can teach him to skate, too. Wouldn't it be ever so much fun if all three of us skated together? Why, we'd be like a regular little family."

Kelsey smiled but kept her thoughts to herself. The idea of Ryan on skates amused her. The thought of holding hands and skating together as a family depressed her. Better to leave the entire topic alone.

Motor purring, the shining blue car glided into the driveway. The garage door slid upward with a quiet rumble. Behind the tinted glass, Ryan was only a tall, masculine shadow.

On the opposite side of the garage, away from the driver's side, Kelsey and Mariah skated slowly up the sidewalk in Ryan's direction. They couldn't see him yet, but they heard the car door slam. He came around the back of the car, a deep frown on his face. Mariah didn't seem to notice. Kelsey definitely did.

Something was wrong. A feeling of dread pulled at her

stomach. She hoped the man in the burn unit hadn't taken a turn for the worse. He had been doing so much better of late.

"Look, Daddy. I can skate." Mariah shook loose from Kelsey and slowly rolled toward her father, bumping into his legs to stop her progress. "This is so much fun," she said, looking up at him, her arms around his knees for support. "Kelsey taught me. Isn't she the most prodigious nanny ever?"

Ryan's frown softened. He went down on one knee and pulled his daughter into a hug. The sight grabbed Kelsey right in the center of her chest, just as it always did when the big tycoon went all mushy with his child.

"You are the most prodigious daughter ever," he said.

"What about Kelsey? Isn't she prodigious, too? I think she is. I think she'd make a remarkable mother, if the two of you would only give the matter some serious thought. It's foolish to look elsewhere when we already have the perfect mommy right here under our roof." She stuck out a pink elbow. "Earlier I took a tumble, but Kelsey caught me. These pads are great. Did you know she was in a Rollerblade club in Seattle?"

"I didn't." He stood, one hand on Mariah's soft, dark curls and turned his attention to the nanny. "I suggest we go inside now. I'd like to talk to Kelsey about something."

The words may have sounded mild, but an undercurrent ran from Ryan to her. Something was wrong indeed. Ryan seethed with some emotion Kelsey did not understand.

Concerned and anxious to know what was going on, she followed him inside.

Mariah, arms out to the sides and holding to any and every thing for balance, wobbled to a chair and began to unlace the skates.

"In my office, please," Ryan said to Kelsey, the command terse and imperious. He angled his head toward the room down the hall.

Mariah caught the tone and glanced from Kelsey to her father. "Daddy?"

He turned toward his daughter. "Run upstairs and put your skates away and then have a snack if you'd like. I'll come up when I'm finished."

Kelsey blinked hard at the strange turn of phrase. Finished with what? Her? What had she done this time?

Without waiting for his daughter's acquiescence, Ryan marched into his office, held the door while Kelsey passed through, and then closed and locked it. Cold fury emanated from him as he turned to glare at her.

Kelsey found her voice. "Is there a problem?"

"A problem? I think so." He raked a hand through his hair, sent it shooting in all directions. The movements were jerky and frustrated. "What in heaven's name did you think you were doing out there?"

The sharp question caught her by surprise. "Today? Outside?"

The cold glare grew hot. "Don't play dumb."

"I'd think that was obvious. I was teaching your daughter to skate." She held both palms up and out in question. What was the big deal?

His jaw flexed. "How can you be competent one day and so irresponsible the next?"

"Look, Ryan, if I've done something wrong, tell me. Teaching Mariah to skate is not irresponsible. She's learning gross motor skills, balance, confidence and getting some much needed exercise. What could possibly be wrong with that? All children love skating."

"It's not Mariah I'm talking about." His voice rose with each word. "Good lord, woman. You're pregnant! What if you'd fallen?"

Oh, for goodness sake. "I'm an experienced skater. And a fall will not kill me."

He blanched. "I won't have it. If you are going to work for me, you will not put yourself in danger."

Kelsey slammed a fist onto one hip. "Don't pull your god complex on me, Ryan. I am an adult who is perfectly capable of making her own decisions."

His eyes widened, his nostrils flared. Kelsey knew she'd pushed the danger button. In a barely controlled voice, he said, "I am your employer. You will do what I say."

This time he'd gone too far. No one, *no one* told her what to do. After the fiasco in Seattle she would never again let anyone have control over her life.

"Excuse me, Mr. Storm," she said, as angry now as he. "You may play high and mighty with the rest of your workers, but not with me. I will do as I please."

"You will do as *I say*." On the last two words, he thrust an index finger in her direction, furious at her insubordination.

Well, she had a little fury in her, too. And it was about to break loose all over his office. "Or what? You'll fire me?"

Two beats passed while the air between them danced with tension. When he spoke, the words were deathly soft. "Maybe I will."

A frisson of anxiety raised up Kelsey's spine. Her head kept telling her to shut-up before she lost the best job she'd ever had, but emotions were running too high. "Then do it."

While he glared at her, hands on hips, Kelsey spun away. In her anger, she forgot about the skates. Moving too quickly, the roller blades sent her sliding forward out of control. She caught a toe on a chair leg and pitched forward. Arms flung outward for balance, she slammed her side against the corner of a desk and started down.

Ryan's strong hands caught her before she hit the floor.

And in the next instant she was on her feet and in his arms.

His chest heaved. His black as onyx eyes raked her face frantically, desperately.

In her own state of fear and confusion, she clung to him. Her side ached. Her pulse pounded in her throat.

But being in Ryan's arms felt terrifyingly right. The memory of that troublesome first kiss came back in vivid detail.

"You drive me crazy," Ryan murmured. "I don't know what to do with you."

"Are you going to fire me?" The words came out in a shaky whisper.

"God help me, I should."

Then with a groan, his mouth crashed down on hers.

CHAPTER TEN

THIS KISS WAS FAR DIFFERENT from that first soft brush of lips. This one was meant to conquer, to control, to lash out whatever frustrations he felt.

Shocked and still fighting mad, Kelsey jerked back.

Instantly, Ryan stopped. Face close to hers, breath to breath, he seemed as disoriented and confused as she. Some nameless emotion spiraled around them, dissipating the hot anger of seconds ago. There was a restlessness in him, in his gaze, in the strong hands pressing at the center of her back, that had nothing to do with anger.

It was a restlessness Kelsey understood very well. She'd felt it, too, though she'd not let herself explore the source.

Now she knew. It was him, Ryan Storm, who'd invaded her mind and her dreams. A man with whom she had no business getting involved. An employer who did not fraternize with employees.

While she considered all the reasons she should pull away and leave this room before she did something foolish and irreversible, Ryan lifted one hand to stroke her cheek. Hard fingertips drifted across her lips and down her throat, rough but tender.

A delicious shiver danced across her skin.

Ryan noticed and smiled.

Kelsey's heart reacted. She smiled back. Ryan must have

taken the smile as a sign of welcome. His mouth claimed hers again, this time in a gentle apology, slow, thoughtful, questioning. More a caress than a kiss, this meeting of lips was so sweet that Kelsey trembled in response.

He claimed she was driving him crazy? She felt exactly the same. But at that moment, the only thing that mattered was being in his embrace.

Pulse thundering, she slid her arms around his neck and pulled him closer, kissing him back with all the emotion boiling up inside her. Her fingers played at the nape of his neck, learning the feel of his skin, the texture of his hair, the heat of him.

For all those times she'd wondered what kind of kisser Ryan Storm would be, now she had her answer. Amazing. Incredible. His warm, supple mouth was a dream come true. There weren't enough superlatives to describe the sensations rippling from his lips through her entire body.

Okay, she admitted it. She'd been wanting this. Wanting him to kiss her again. Wanting to feel admired and desired by the man who occupied her thoughts day in and day out.

Something was happening between them, something less than prudent, but Kelsey could no more stop the plunge of emotion than she could stop the inevitable birth of her child.

She was falling in love with her boss.

Somewhere in the spiral of sensation, the thought smacked her upside the head. She, who had sworn off driven men forever, was falling in love with the darling of Dallas.

And that could not happen.

With more willpower than she thought possible, Kelsey dropped her arms to her sides and separated her body from his, ending the beautiful kiss. Everything in her cried out to be crushed against him still, but she knew better. She would not be a fool again.

She tried to pull away, but Ryan did not release her. Hands

gripping her upper arms, he held her upright, still concerned she would fall. He couldn't know how right he was, though the roller blades were not the problem. Her knees trembled fiercely and weakness had invaded her body.

She needed to get out of this office. To get away and think.

She could feel his eyes on her, compelling her to look at him. She couldn't.

What did one say to a boss who had just yelled at her and then kissed her cross-eyed? A boss with whom she could not fall in love.

"I should go check on Mariah."

The words came out in a husky whisper, betraying her tumultuous emotions.

"Yes." Yet, he did not release her. "Kelsey."

She looked up. If the man apologized again or used the word fraternize, she'd be tempted to do something awful.

"Don't you dare say that shouldn't have happened," she blurted. "I already know that, but it did. So we just have to forget about it and move on. I assure you I did not take it seriously. You're my boss. I'm the employee. A simple little kiss didn't mean a thing. We've kissed before and neither of us died. It's over, done, never to be mentioned again."

Kelsey knew she was rambling. Panic did that to a person. But somehow she had to let him off the hook before he started apologizing again. She also had to keep him from knowing the truth— she was falling in love with him. If he knew, he'd fire her in an instant. With the baby only weeks away, she couldn't let that happen.

Ryan's dark eyebrows plunged together. Carefully, he loosened his grip on her shoulders and stepped back, leaving her to stand on her own. "Sit down before you fall."

She knew he was right, though the weakness irked her no end. As wobbly as a broken top, she slithered into the nearest chair.

"Mariah will be wondering what's keeping us," she said.

"Mariah is fine. I think we should talk."

"We'll only fight."

"We wouldn't if you'd obey orders."

"Obey orders?" What was he talking about? What orders? And did Ryan Storm kiss all his employees who didn't jump at his command? "This is not the twelfth century, Mr. Storm, and I am not a serf. I don't even know what you were so angry about."

"I wasn't angry." He blew out an exasperated sigh. "I was—" He stopped, blinked twice in bewilderment, and finally finished with, "You can't seem to take proper care of yourself. It drives me to distraction."

The shift in topics took her by surprise, but she went with it, though her lips still ached deliciously and her head couldn't stop thinking about his warm mouth on hers. "I take excellent care of myself."

She ate healthy meals, exercised and paid regular visits to the obstetricians. What more was there?

"Not from my point of view." He raked a hand over the top of his hair. By now, the usually perfect grooming was a sexy, rumpled mess. Kelsey shivered with the need to smooth it down and feel the soft coarseness against her fingertips once again.

"Look, Kelsey, you're pregnant." As if she didn't know. "The baby is due—" He stopped, stymied. "When *is* the baby due?"

"Six weeks." She tenderly placed both hands on the growing mound beneath her heart.

Ryan closed his eyes. A shudder ran through him. "Six weeks. Good lord, woman, you have no business on a pair of roller skates. Something terrible could have happened."

"Even so, that would be my concern."

"You're in my employ. I'm responsible for your well-being."

Suddenly, Ryan's behavior began to make a sick sort of sense.

Just as he'd taken responsibility for the burned workmen, he felt responsible for her. As an employee.

Boy, was she stupid. Stupid and confused.

Ryan was only worried about her health.

And yet, he'd kissed her. Again.

What kind of employer did that?

At midnight, Ryan prowled the house still grappling with the events of the afternoon. The upstairs had long since darkened and grown quiet but he had no hope of sleep. Kelsey Slater, boy hater, worried him to no end.

He didn't know what was wrong with him. Every time Kelsey was near, he alternated between wanting to protect her, wanting to kiss her and wanting her to go away. Most evenings, he kept his emotions under control, but this evening when he'd turned into the drive and seen her wobbling down the walk on skates, his heart had stopped. Gripped with terror, maybe he'd over-reacted. Maybe he shouldn't have come across so imperious, commanding her to obey him like some sultan with his love slave.

The unfortunate term ricocheted through his brain and set off the most disturbingly sensual images. He battled them back. That was the problem of late. Kelsey made him think about things he kept buried. Things like love and sex, a wife and a mother, a friend and a lover.

He paced into the kitchen and opened the refrigerator for another glass of wine.

After Amanda died, he'd determined never to be so vulnerable again. Love was wonderful, but it could also devastate.

The chardonnay gurgled softly as he poured, the fruity aroma drifting to his nostrils.

He liked Kelsey. Might as well admit that much. He liked

being in her company. Since he'd begun arriving home in time for dinner, he looked forward to talking to her, to hearing about her and Mariah's day together. And she listened to him discuss his business with rapt attention and encouragement that made him feel like a man who could conquer the world.

Why had he kissed her? He was still bewildered by that. And yet, those few minutes in her arms had been right and good in a way he had never experienced. He'd felt almost whole, something he hadn't felt since Amanda had died. Since he'd let her die.

There it was again to haunt him. Kelsey was pregnant. Had some cosmic force sent her to punish him for the wrong he'd done to Amanda? Seeing her on those skates had been torment, all right. And when she'd stumbled into his desk, terror had ripped into him with the force of a buzz saw.

That must be why he'd kissed her—an overreaction from fear.

He knocked back a gulp of wine, barely noting the sweet-tart taste.

Who was he kidding? Something was happening between him and Kelsey, a widow still grieving her husband. He felt like a vulture for taking advantage.

Disgusted with himself, Ryan took the refilled wine glass into the living area. As he passed the staircase, he noticed a light coming from Kelsey's end of the hallway.

Setting the glass aside, he waited at the bottom step, listening. He caught the faint sound of someone moving around.

Was everything okay up there?

When the light didn't go off after several minutes, tension tightened the muscles of his shoulders. Kelsey had seemed fine when they'd jointly put Mariah to bed. Snuggle time had become a tradition he looked forward to, and if the nanny was part of the reason, he couldn't say he was sorry. Tonight she'd tried to weasel out of the ritual, but he'd insisted, hoping a little togetherness would erase any residual tension between them. It hadn't.

A door opened. More light spread down the hallway.

A prickle of worry lifted the hair on the back of his neck. Kelsey was generally long asleep by now. Something wasn't right.

Had she been hurt when she stumbled against his desk? She claimed not to be, but why was she moving around at this time of night?

Maybe she'd decided to pack up and leave. Maybe he'd pushed her over the limit today.

No, she wouldn't leave without warning, especially now with the baby so close. Would she?

Hand on the polished banister, Ryan started up the steps. Kelsey, a hand to her stomach, stepped into sight at the top of the stairs.

Eyes wide, she looked pale and frightened.

"Kelsey?" he said. The prickle of worry turned to downright fear.

She paused, leaned for a moment against the railing, and bracketed her belly with both hands. Her labored breath reached his ears.

Ryan covered the remaining stairs in two leaps.

"What's wrong?" he asked, afraid to touch her, afraid not to.

She looked at him, beseeching. "I think I'm in labor."

Pure unadulterated terror slammed into Ryan and knocked him momentarily breathless. The roar in his head produced a vision of Amanda, on the floor, motionless and pale.

A tiny sound from Kelsey snapped him back to the present. "Will you take me to the hospital?" she whispered.

Heart ricocheting against his ribcage, Ryan swept her into his arms and carried her down the stairs where he gently deposited her on the sofa. He perched one hip on the edge next to her. "How long has this been going on?"

"A couple of hours."

"And you're just now letting me know?"

"I didn't want to bother you. I thought it would go away." Tears welled in her eyes as another pain took over. When the moment passed, she said, "Ryan, it's too early."

He knew that. Grimly, he grabbed for the telephone. "I'll call an ambulance."

"No." She stopped him with a touch on the arm. "The ambulance scares me. You take me. Please."

Her pleading was his undoing. He'd heard that sound in a woman's voice before and ignored it.

"I'll wake Mariah."

She nodded, her lips trembling. The sight tore into Ryan's conscience. This was his fault. He shouldn't have upset her. He shouldn't have yelled at her. Most of all, he shouldn't have kissed her.

Adrenaline on overload, he raced up the stairs and met Mariah coming down, dragging a stuffed animal. "Daddy? What's all the noise?"

"Kelsey's not feeling well." He forced a false sense of calm into the explanation. "We're going to drive out to the hospital so the doctor can check her."

"Is she going to die like Mommy?"

The question was a punch in the gut. Bile rose in his throat. "No, peanut. Kelsey will be okay." Please God, let her be okay. "It's just a check-up. You know about check-ups."

Even sleepy-headed, his daughter was not a dummy. "In the night?"

"Yes, in the night. Now go get dressed. We need to hurry."

Ryan drove like a shark through the lighted streets of Dallas, slicing between cars and big rigs with deadly precision. Mariah curled under her blanket in the seat next to him, awake but unusually quiet. Kelsey was in the back, her restless movements the only indication of her discomfort. She didn't utter a sound, which only scared him more. Amanda had been silent, too.

After what seemed like an eternity, they reached the emergency room. Refusing to give in to panic for her sake, he gingerly helped Kelsey out of the car and into a wheelchair. White-faced, she gripped his hand. "Ryan?"

He wanted so badly to hold her and make everything all right. All he could do was offer platitudes.

"Shh," he said, smoothing a hand down her soft hair. "Everything's okay now. They'll take good care of you."

She managed a brave, if wobbly, smile before the nurse whisked her away, leaving him and Mariah to wait and worry.

Well, he worried. Mariah chatted with the night nurses and the other people in the waiting area. Several times, sirens wailed in the distance and then grew closer and closer until the back doors burst open and medical personnel rushed in with the wounded and bleeding.

This wasn't the kind of place he wanted Mariah to be. He remembered all too clearly the frantic race to save Amanda and Mariah. The hours of waiting and praying, followed by days and months of devastation.

He remembered, too, the fire that had brought him and his men here. Jamie still battled for his life in the burn unit. Though Storm International was paying the medical bills and sending each of Jamie's paychecks to his wife without fail, no amount of money could buy back the man's health.

That was the curse of the rich. Money could buy everything except the things that mattered most.

Elbows on his thighs, Ryan leaned his forehead onto the heels of his hands. God, he hated this place.

Mariah came over and rested a hand on his knee. "Are you worried about Kelsey's baby?"

He straightened. No use scaring his child.

"Not too much." Liar. His guts gnawed with acid indigestion. His neck muscles were tight enough to snap. He wasn't worried. He was about to implode.

"Good." His little optimist climbed up on his lap and patted his cheeks. "I was scared at first, but now I'm not. I felt the baby moving around tonight when we were reading. The nurse says that means she's okay. It's a girl you know—the sister I've been wanting. Kelsey let me put my hand on her tummy and feel. It's pretty interesting. You should try it sometime."

Not on his life. What he should do is figure out a way to let Kelsey go. But if he did, she'd be alone. He didn't like that idea either.

After more than an hour, a door swung outward and the obstetrician on call came into the waiting area. Ryan rose to greet him, prepared for the worst. It wouldn't be the first time.

The balding doctor smiled. "Everything is fine. You can take her home."

"Take her home?" Ryan couldn't quite grasp what he was hearing. "But what about the baby?"

"The contractions have stopped. False labor. It's quite common in first-time mothers, a prelude to the big event."

The breath Ryan had been holding whooshed out. He almost collapsed from relief.

"See, Daddy?" Mariah said, tugging at his hand. "Everything is rosy. Come on. Let's get Kelsey and go home. You look positively exhausted."

CHAPTER ELEVEN

FOR THE NEXT COUPLE of days, Kelsey took things easier than usual, embarrassed to have made such a fuss. According to the doctor, lots of women experienced false labor, and he'd tried to educate her on the difference. She wished she'd known before, because Ryan had become more overbearing than ever. He telephoned no less than five times a day, usually more. He demanded that she stay close to the town house and do nothing more strenuous than sit beside his daughter while she studied.

His behavior was both endearing and maddening.

At the moment, he was tinkering with something in the garage after complaining that she should have allowed the housekeeper to cook dinner instead of doing it herself.

But Kelsey liked to cook and, according to the doctor, false labor was no reason to curtail her usual activities. Irregular contractions in the last weeks of pregnancy were normal, a warmup exercise for the real thing. Ryan had heard the doctor's instructions but, as usual, preferred his own interpretation. She'd made a trip to the E.R. and that was proof enough for Mr. Overprotective-know-it-all.

"Come on, Mariah," she said, pushing off the sofa that had become her prison. "Let's make something fun for dessert."

Mariah looked up from a kid's book on pregnancy. Since the E.R. episode, she'd become as obsessed as her father. "Shouldn't you be resting?"

"Look, little miss, don't you start, too. Your daddy is already driving me crazy."

"That's because he cares about you."

Kelsey refused to let the comment move her. Ryan did care, but he cared about all his employees. That much was clear from his vigilant attention to the burned workmen and their families. She was different in only one way. She was underfoot all the time. He had no choice but to monitor her comings and goings. If she enjoyed his attention a little too much, that was her fault, not his.

Waddling into the kitchen, Mariah in tow, she said, "Ever made ice cream in a zippie bag?"

Mariah's dark curls bounced as she shook her head. "No, but it sounds wonderful."

"Easy, too. Did you know ice cream is a colloid?" Knowing Mariah loved big words, she explained the meaning as they assembled the simple ingredients. In minutes, Mariah sat at the bar, shaking a giant plastic baggie of ice and salt back and forth while Kelsey worked at the stove.

The door to the garage opened and Ryan sauntered in. Kelsey refused to acknowledge the happy dance that rushed through her blood every time he appeared. Today he was dressed in an old sweat shirt and soft faded jeans, and Kelsey found them every bit as attractive as an Armani suit.

He tapped Mariah on the nose, threw a leg over a chair, and without prelude, said to Kelsey, "I've been thinking. You should move into my bedroom."

Her stomach, big as it was, jumped into her throat. "What?"

"You shouldn't be climbing those stairs so much. You can move into my room."

She had to ask the obvious. "And where will you sleep?"

His skin darkened. He apparently hadn't considered the wording of his request. "Let me rephrase. We should trade rooms."

"No." She turned back to the double boiler where the scent of chocolate tantalized her.

"Be sensible."

"Ryan, stop hovering. I am not going to have a baby on your kitchen floor or in your car or in your bedroom. The doctor says the baby should arrive on time as planned, and there is no reason to expect that to change. Climbing stairs is good exercise." She pointed a cooking spoon at him. "Furthermore, I'm going shopping tomorrow."

His scowl said it all. "You are not."

She tilted her head in a look of warning.

Ryan didn't get the message. "Make a list. I'll have someone shop for you."

"I *want* to shop. Shopping is a girl thing, remember? We like walking around for hours in malls and other stores. It's our idea of fun."

He grimaced at the very idea. "Anything I can do to change your mind?"

"Nope. Here. Taste this. I think it's cool enough." She stuck a wooden spoon against his lips, one hand beneath to catch any drips.

Eyes holding hers, he placed his wonderful mouth over the tip of the spoon and supped. A zing of awareness sizzled between them, and Kelsey was sorry she'd offered. This whole issue of being acutely conscious of Ryan every time he was in the room had to stop. Really, it did.

"Good stuff," he murmured. "What is it?"

"Mariah's science project."

He tilted back in mock horror. "Am I going to die?"

"Daddy!" Mariah, who had been intently shaking the plastic bag of homemade ice cream, protested. "This is research."

"Ah, I see. You're researching methods to poison your dear old daddy?"

Mariah giggled. "No, silly. Kelsey is making fudge sauce and I'm making ice cream. See?" Oven mitts on her hands to protect them from the cold, she held the large baggie up for his examination. "Salt lowers the freezing point of ice. Kelsey says the heat is transferred from the milk to the melting ice and that makes the cream freeze. Isn't that positively amazing?"

"Positively." Eyes twinkling, he looked at Kelsey. "When can I eat it?"

"When you stop nagging me to take it easy."

His levity faded. "Your health is not a joking matter."

"Loosen up, Ryan." She helped Mariah transfer the now-frozen concoction into bowls. "Life is too short to fret over every little thing."

Mariah topped each dip with the fudge sauce and carried a bowl to her father. "Eat fast. It's melting."

The three of them settled at the bar to enjoy Mariah's treat. Ryan made so many sounds of approval, they all began to giggle, but Mariah glowed from the praise.

And if Ryan's gaze clashed with Kelsey's a few times too many and if the mood felt a little too flirtatious, she refused to read anything into it. Not one single thing.

"You're what?" Kelsey was sure she'd heard him wrong. Ryan had gone to work as usual the next morning but now, just before noon, he was back at the town house.

"I'm going shopping with you. We'll all have lunch together somewhere."

That sounded better than it should. "What about work?"

"I'm taking the afternoon off."

"You never take time off."

He shrugged. "Then I must have plenty of vacation leave built up."

"It's your company."

"There is that. I can take off if I want to."

"I think I'm going to faint."

"If you do, I won't let you go shopping."

Ah, so that was it. He wasn't going along because he wanted her company. He was playing macho protector again.

"Did anyone ever tell you what a pain you can be?"

He grinned, unrepentant. "All the time." Holding an elbow out, he said, "Shall we shop?"

She rolled her eyes and took his arm. "Come on, Mariah, I guess we're stuck with him."

Mariah, of course, was delighted. "I'm hungry. May we eat first?"

"Food first. Shop later. Sounds like a great idea to me," Ryan said.

Kelsey made a rude noise. "Oh, go get in the car."

Ryan laughed, and suddenly the shopping trip seemed even more exciting.

All the way to the restaurant, Mariah bounced and chattered, overstimulated to have her daddy along. Poor kid, this was a treat of the first order.

At the small, trendy bistro, Ryan's request for a specific, cozy table toward the back was granted within minutes. That he'd been here before was obvious from the extra attention given him by the manager and wait staff.

Even in the lunch crowd of businessmen, the restaurant's atmosphere was intimate, romantic even, and Kelsey found her thoughts running a little wild.

Ryan, handsome and solicitous, paid her far too much attention. And fool that she was, Kelsey reveled in every touch, every word, every glance.

By the time lunch was over, she was fighting to remember that this was business, not a date.

"Sure you're feeling all right?" Ryan asked for the tenth time as they left the eatery. "No pain? No twinges?"

"Only the pain of overeating," she said.

"Me, too." He rubbed his taut belly and groaned. Today, he wore his usual dark business suit with the perfectly tailored jacket open over a maroon shirt. He looked more delicious than the food.

"Shopping will burn it off."

"I was hoping you'd forgotten about that."

"Ha. Fat chance."

Mariah, who was holding her daddy's hand, asked, "Is that a pun?"

Kelsey patted her oversized belly. "I think it could be."

"We can walk to the Galleria if you're up to it," Ryan said, naming the exclusive glass-topped shopping center that housed over two hundred of the best and most expensive stores in Dallas.

Kelsey swallowed back a protest. The Galleria was a bit too pricey for her pocketbook but she could window-shop and dream. "Sure."

They walked the two blocks and in minutes were beneath the glass dome amidst shops the like of Versace and Tiffany's. They roamed in and out of each one, browsing. At a children's store Mariah tried on new boots. At a chocolatier, Ryan bought a bag of sumptuous treats to share. Mostly, they browsed the baby items which were the purpose of the trip in the first place.

At one store, a pink-and-green layette caught Kelsey's eye.

Matching bedding lined a white crib with arched end pieces. The sleigh crib was exactly what she would have bought a year ago before the world went crazy.

"You like this?" Ryan asked.

"Love it."

"Buy it. We'll have them deliver it to the house."

"Mmm. I don't think so." She didn't want to tell him that money was the issue. Instead she joked, "You're just trying to get me to buy something so we can leave."

He laughed and held up both hands in surrender. "Guilty as charged. Buy the whole store, and let's go somewhere for ice cream."

Longing to give her baby beautiful things, she nevertheless maneuvered away from the tempting furniture. "One more store and we'll leave. I promise."

"But you haven't bought anything."

"I haven't found exactly what I want yet." This much was true. She wanted beautiful things at a very bargain price, even if she couldn't find them.

Ryan shook his head in mock despair. "Women."

As they exited the store with Mariah between them, she suddenly grasped each of their hands and pulled them together until Kelsey's fingers were wrapped in Ryan's.

"There. That's more like it," she said with satisfaction. While the two adults looked at each other in surprise, Little Miss Matchmaker clasped Ryan's opposite hand and started off again, humming happily.

Ryan shrugged. "She's incorrigible." But he didn't pull away.

The warmth of his skin against Kelsey's elicited an amazing internal reaction. Excitement, anxiety and pure happiness. All this from holding a man's hand.

"If she's incorrigible, it's your fault," Kelsey teased.

Ryan wasn't to be outdone. "I hired you to fix the problem."

"She's smarter than both of us."

"There is that."

So they walked hand in hand through the mall, window shopping, laughing, talking. Ryan was a good date. If this was a date, which it wasn't, though it felt very much like one.

As they passed a men's shop, Kelsey pointed. "You would look great in that sweater."

"You think?" He seemed pleased that she would think of him.

"Absolutely. Why don't you try it?"

"This is supposed to be *your* shopping trip."

"And I want to see you in blue cashmere."

"Then lead the way. Your wish is my command."

Inside the exclusive store, the sales clerks were instantly aware of Ryan Storm's presence.

"Mr. Storm, it's a pleasure to see you again." The clerk turned his attention to Kelsey and Mariah. "And is this Mrs. Storm?"

A hot blush raced over Kelsey's face. Her freckles must be flashing like a neon sigh.

Smooth as silk, Ryan said, "This is Kelsey Mason, a good friend, and you've met my daughter, Mariah."

A friend. He hadn't called her "the nanny" or an employee. He'd called her his friend.

The clerk simpered appropriately and the uncomfortable moment passed, but Kelsey couldn't get the thought out of her mind.

When Ryan came out of the dressing room, blue cashmere against his darkly handsome skin, Kelsey thought he was the handsomest man she'd ever seen. From the admiring looks he received, others must have shared her opinion.

"You have to buy that."

He preened a bit, making her smile. "Like it?"

She liked what was in it. "Yes, I do. What do you think, Mariah?"

"I think my daddy is the best-looking older man in Texas," she said and then appeared bewildered when Ryan grimaced and Kelsey laughed.

After Ryan bought the sweater and they left the store, Kelsey teased, "Come on, old guy, I'll help you to the car."

"Maybe you should hold my hand," Ryan answered, dark eyes sparkling. "I'm feeling pretty feeble."

"Poor thing," she countered, but gladly took his hand again. "How about some ice cream to strengthen your old bones?"

"Now you're talking. There's a creamery on the other level."

Just to see his reaction, she said, "Or we could always go ice skating." The Galleria was built in the round with an ice-skating rink in the center floor.

Ryan shot her a scowl. "Don't even think about it."

She laughed at him, feeling happy. "Stuffed shirt."

"Risk taker."

"And you aren't? Good grief, Ryan, you buy and sell and speculate in international markets on a daily basis. That's pretty risky if you ask me."

"Calculated risks are different. I know what I'm doing."

"Which means if I choose to skate I don't know what I'm doing?"

"Not while expecting a baby," he clarified.

"Okay, okay. I get the message. No more wild and crazy sports activities until after the baby comes."

"Good. I was thinking of hiring a keeper for you."

From his expression, Kelsey thought he might not be kidding!

They'd reached the ice-cream shop by now, finding the place mildly crowded for wintertime but managed to secure a table.

"I ordered cookies and cream," Mariah announced. "With gummy bears on top." She took an enormous bite.

"Interesting choice," Kelsey said. In ice cream, Mariah was no different than any other child—candy and cookies reigned supreme. "Mine is double dark chocolate with hot fudge sauce."

Ryan's eyes widened. "Sounds dangerous."

"Not at all. But a woman *without* chocolate is dangerous." She scooped a spoonful. Waving it back and forth under her nose, she closed her eyes and breathed in the aroma. "As long as we have it, we're pussycats."

"I'll have to remember that."

"Brain freeze, brain freeze!" Mariah moaned as she thunked her cup onto the table top and grabbed her head with both hands. Eyes squinched tightly, her face reddened in pain. Kelsey felt sorry for her, but knew there was little to be done for an ice-cream headache. When the pain subsided, Mariah blew out a deep breath. "Thank goodness that's over."

"I'm sorry, sweetness."

Mariah, resilient as always, went right back to the ice cream. "What causes that?"

"I don't know. We'll have to look it up."

"Maybe we can discover a cure and become world famous."

"Try smaller bites," Ryan suggested, indicating the huge spoon of ice cream Mariah was about to shovel into her mouth.

"Okay."

Once the headache had passed and Mariah was settled into her treat, Kelsey indicated Ryan's sundae with whipped cream and a cherry.

"What's your concoction?"

He dipped a spoonful and held it aloft. "The Elvis special, peanut butter and banana."

Kelsey smiled. "You're kidding."

He slipped the spoon into his mouth and made a sound of approval.

"Try a bite. Elvis knew his stuff." He leaned across the table and tapped her lips with his spoon.

The mood was light and fun so Kelsey opened her mouth, but as soon as the spoon touched her lips, her mind went crazy. Ryan's gaze was locked on hers, a quizzical tilt to his own luscious lips. Lips that had just touched this spoon. Lips that had kissed hers with wild abandon gone soft and sweet.

A tingle of awareness arced across the table.

To cover her discomfiture, Kelsey swallowed the Elvis special and said, "Makes me want to sing 'Hound Dog.'"

Ryan grinned and touched her nose. "Your freckles are cute when you blush."

"Ahh, the bane of my existence."

"Why? I like them."

A warm glow filled her. He'd complimented her cooking and her teaching, but this was the first personal compliment. She liked it a little too much.

"I was teased a lot in school," she admitted. "Kids claimed they would rub off or that they were a contagious pox. Add to that my dark red hair and I heard all the taunts."

"I always thought your hair was pretty, even in high school."

He did? "And all this time, I thought you were asleep."

"I was. The warm glow of your hair woke me up in time to take a test or to avoid a detention slip."

At the silly joke, she rolled her eyes. "Ha-ha. Very funny. Now I understand why you didn't play sports. Everyone thought you would have been awesome in football."

He shrugged. "It wasn't for lack of wanting to play. But I had to work."

"Why?" She stirred the hot fudge sauce around in the plastic container. "Were things that difficult at home?"

He licked the end of his spoon and went back for another

scoop. "Life was tough. No dad around most of the time. Mom was worn down and sickly, though she did her best. As the oldest of three and the only male, I had little choice but to take up the slack. No work, no eat, as the saying goes. You were lucky to be born with the proverbial silver spoon in your mouth."

The idea startled her. "We were an average family. I didn't have a silver spoon."

"It looked silver from my side of town."

She supposed it had. "Funny how life changes things."

"Not life. Long hours. Hard work. A bit of luck."

"You don't have to work so hard anymore, Ryan. You could relax a little, take up a hobby."

"I've been thinking about it." His gaze flicked up to hers. "Lately."

Was he saying he had been listening all those times she'd encouraged him to spend more time with his daughter? Or was the comment something more personal?

Kelsey cast the last thought to the wind. Ryan called her friend, but that was the end of any relationship.

"What would you do if you had all the spare time in the world?" she asked. "Golf? Hot cars?"

"The only golf I've played has been for making business deals. I like it though. And I take in a Mavericks game now and then. When I was a teenager, I liked tinkering with my old truck, although that was more necessity than hobby. What about you?"

"Oh, I like lots of things. Antiques, cross-stitch, dance."

"Don't forget roller skating," he said, eyes twinkling.

"I play the piano, too. Bet you didn't know that."

"We'll have to buy one for the house." He probably would, too. "What about sailing? Your husband was a yacht dealer, right?"

Kelsey suppressed a shudder. "Picture this, a yachting enthusiast whose wife is afraid of water."

"Seriously?" He pushed his empty dish aside.

"Mark loved the water and boats, but I seldom went out with him." A fact that annoyed her late husband and caused a rift in their marriage early on. Eventually, he stopped asking her to join his outings, which were many. After his death, she learned that he had found other women who were more than willing to accompany a successful yacht dealer all over the world.

"So that's why you weren't on the yacht when the accident occurred."

Among other reasons, one being the huge fight they'd had three days before when she'd announced the pregnancy. Mark was so angry, he hadn't even said goodbye before leaving for Greece. The marriage had long been in trouble, but that night she'd known it was over. She just hadn't realized the end would be death instead of divorce.

Deep in thought, Kelsey stared into her melting chocolate and didn't say anything. It still hurt to know she'd been a fool and that Mark had cared so little for her or their baby.

Ryan touched the top of her hand. "Sorry. Bad topic. I didn't mean to spoil our day with a sad memory."

She managed a smile. "Nothing will spoil this. I'm having a great time."

"Good. Me, too."

Mariah popped up. "Me three, but next time I think the two of you should go out alone."

Both adults turned to stare at the precocious child. In response, she placed both hands on the table and leaned forward.

"People, people, people," she said with adult patience. "I need a mommy. I want a mommy. When are you going to get the message?"

CHAPTER TWELVE

TWO DAYS LATER, MARIAH'S words still played in Kelsey's head. They'd had a wonderful time at the Galleria, or at least she had, but after Mariah's comment, a reserve had risen between her and Ryan like a retaining wall.

Poor little Mariah. She wanted a mother so badly. But Ryan was no more in the market for a wife than Kelsey was for a husband. A pregnant woman had no business even thinking such things. Ryan was not interested in her as a person.

That's why, when the enormous delivery truck arrived late one afternoon, she was so surprised. Mariah hopped around with excitement as the workmen first unloaded an exquisite piano. If she hadn't been so pregnant, Kelsey might have hopped around, too. Her fingers fairly itched to play again. The piano would be a lovely addition to Ryan's massive, mostly unused formal living room.

But it was the rest of the furniture that shocked her to pieces.

The men carted crate after crate of baby furniture and clothing up the stairs to the bare room Ryan had offered as a nursery. In the weeks since then, she'd painted the walls a barely there shade of green and had begun filling a small chest with a few necessities: diapers, blankets, onesies.

"Mr. Storm says we're to set this up for you wherever and however you want it."

"I can do it myself," she said, still too overwhelmed to think straight. Should she allow Ryan to do this?

"We have our orders."

She imagined they did. And she also knew there was little she could do to stop them.

She could, however, have a long, stern conversation with Mr. Storm. She was not a charity case. She could take care of her baby. In fact, if the insurance company ever declared Mark legally dead, she and baby would do nicely.

She shuddered at the depressing thought. How terrible to have to declare a man dead so she could move on with her life.

As the deliverers groaned and sweated up the stairs for the last time, Ryan strode into the house. One look at her mutinous expression and he held up one hand in a stop sign. "Before you start arguing, forget it. It's done."

"You shouldn't have. When I admired this layette at the Galleria, I never dreamed you'd do such a thing."

They stood in the foyer with the front door open. A breeze circled in around them. Kelsey crossed her arms against the chill.

Ryan pushed the door shut with one foot, then tugged her hand loose and pulled her toward the warmer living room.

"Look, Kelsey, let's be honest. You've admitted you're in debt. I don't mean to pry, but it's obvious you can't buy the things you need and want for the baby. I can."

"Buying for my baby is not your responsibility."

His appraisal turned as cool as the wind in the foyer. "All right then, consider the furniture a bonus for a job well-done."

Exasperated, she said, "You've never said I'm doing a good job."

"Sure I have." He stopped and turned, hands on hips. "Haven't I?"

With a wry laugh, she shook her head. "You have now."

And her chest swelled with the knowledge that he was pleased.

Overhead, something thumped and thudded as the workmen moved around. Gnawing her bottom lip, she looked upward. What were they doing?

"I really should go up there."

He lifted his hands. "Go then."

She started up the stairs only to realize he was right behind her. They met the workmen coming down. Two carried the now-empty cardboard cartons, folded flat.

"All set, Mr. Storm, unless the lady wants us to rearrange something."

"I'd rather do it myself," she said, knowing Ryan would protest.

Ryan took the offered invoice.

"We'll take care of things from here," he told the men, and they thundered down the steps and out the door.

Kelsey was beside herself with both excitement and discomfort. She was getting far too comfortable here in Ryan's home. And now, with the baby only weeks away and a nursery to be set up, the nesting instinct grew stronger every day. It would be easy to pretend this was her home and her family.

As she entered the newly furnished room, tears sprang to her eyes. She pressed a hand to her throat and stood speechless. At last, her precious baby would have a bed to call her own, even if the gorgeous sleigh crib was purchased by someone else.

Ryan stood against the doorframe, arms folded, looking anxious. "Do you like the furniture or not?"

Kelsey nodded, struggling for the right words to say. The last thing she wanted to do was break down and cry in front of him, but stress and rampant hormones wreaked havoc with her emotions. Toss Ryan's kindness in with the perfect layette for her baby, and Kelsey was a mess.

"I love it." She stroked a hand over the smooth, beautiful wood of the crib. Turning to look at him, her eyes swam. "You know I love it."

And she loved him even more for thinking to do such a thing.

All the irritation seeped from him. His shoulders relaxed. Had he really been worried that she wouldn't like it? He came forward and took her in his arms, pulling her close. Overflowing with emotion, she went gladly.

"I wanted to do this, Kelsey," he whispered against her hair. "Buying things for you makes me happy. Don't be angry."

"I'm not. I'm happy, too." She was a little afraid of what was happening to her heart, but definitely happy. "Oh, Ryan, you're too good to me."

"Impossible."

Basking in the sweet moment, she let him hold her while she breathed in the essence that was only Ryan Storm. Tough but urbane. Successful, but still the wild, hungry boy from the wrong side of town. Ryan was a man of fascinating contrasts.

She could have stayed there in his arms forever, but the baby had different ideas. The little one began to thrash and kick until Ryan tilted back.

"Are you okay?" His concern became a puzzling look of fear. What was it about her pregnancy that bothered him so much?

She laughed. "Perfectly. Miss America in there doesn't like to be crowded."

He stepped away, leaving a vacuum in his place. She wished him back, foolish woman that she was.

To hide her longing, Kelsey began to explore the room, exclaiming over each delicate outfit in the layette, touching the changing table, trying out the rocker. He couldn't have chosen anything she'd love more.

Ryan watched her with thoughtful, sometimes amused eyes. He was proud of himself, she could tell, and she wasn't about to take that from him. Giving her this gift really had made him happy.

"Is there anything else you need for the baby?"

"Not that I can see. You've thought of everything."

"I wish I could take credit but I left most of the choices to the experts."

The furniture was unpacked and set up, but the linens, decorations and clothing were still in boxes.

"I can't wait to see how this all looks."

He grabbed a box and ripped back the packing tape. "No time like the present. I'll help."

His enthusiasm amused her. She wrinkled her nose at him. "You just want to stick around and be bossy."

Eyes dancing, he didn't look the least bit sorry. "Busted."

They both chuckled and got to work. Kelsey unzipped a plastic bag containing crib linens and held the soft fabric against her cheek. The nursery-rhyme motif was going to look adorable. Her little girl was going to look adorable and feel so wonderfully loved—even if she didn't have a daddy.

They worked companionably and more than once stopped to show one another some little garment or item. Over and over again, Kelsey opened a box or a bag and exclaimed with pleasure at the treasure within. Each time, Ryan laughed or joked and looked proudly amused by her enthusiastic response.

The notion drifted through Kelsey's mind more than once that this was the way life should be between a man and a woman about to have a baby. Only this baby wasn't Ryan's, and he wasn't her man.

And the reminder was far more painful than she wanted to admit.

Occasionally they paused to discuss the best place for an accessory or a wall hanging. Once or twice a friendly argument arose and they ended up laughing like loons.

Mariah roamed in and out of the nursery, losing interest after a while. Before long, the tinkle of piano keys drifted up the stairs.

"Looks like we may be trading the dulcimer for piano lessons," Ryan said, cocking his head to listen.

"Maybe she'll play both." Kelsey picked up a counting-sheep wall hanging in soft shades of pink and green. "This is beautiful."

"I thought you'd like it."

"Did you pick this yourself?"

Looking both pleased and self-conscious, he nodded. "Yeah."

Putting aside a white-fringed lamp of Little Bo Peep, he leaned over her shoulder and touched the plaque. "There's a place for the baby's name here. We can have that added later."

She ran her finger back and forth over the spot and then glanced back at Ryan. "My baby is lucky that you came into our lives. Very lucky. Blessed, really."

Heart full, she didn't know how to express what his kindness meant to her.

Ryan shifted away and swallowed, apparently uncomfortable with the emotional compliment. She was sorry about that. She liked having him close and relaxed.

"Have you chosen a name yet?"

"Mariah and I made a list." She pointed to a spot on the wall. "Let's hang this here."

Ryan took a hammer from the small tool chest he'd carried up from the garage. "I can imagine my daughter's suggestions."

Kelsey handed him a picture hanger. "Somehow I can't get on board with a name like Persephone."

A startled laugh burst from him. He lowered the hammer to look at her. "Good lord. What else?"

She grinned. "Brace yourself for this one. Aphrodesia. I don't think she knows the meaning yet."

He shook his head and laughed. "My daughter. What a mind. Please don't let her read any more mythology until after the baby arrives."

He turned back to the wall, found the stud and tapped the hanger into place.

Kelsey stood close, watching him work, the hammer at the ready whenever he was.

"I told her we might settle for something a bit less dramatic. Perhaps Alison or Amanda."

Just that quick, all joviality seeped out of him. He lowered the hammer and stared at her, bleak and lost.

"Amanda," he said quietly, voice ragged with despair. "Amanda was my wife."

Ryan heard the sucking intake of Kelsey's breath. He felt her small, warm hand on his arm. She moved closer as if her sympathy could protect him from his own guilt. It couldn't. He wanted a lot of things from Kelsey, but sympathy wasn't one of them.

"You've never told me about her," she said, pushing in where he seldom let anyone go. But that was Kelsey. She didn't know her power yet, but she'd slipped under his radar a long time ago. He thought about her all day long, hurried home each evening to hear her laugh. Buying the baby furniture had been his penance for causing her to go into false labor. It had also been fun. He'd been anxious to see her reaction, and after the expected argument, he'd been proud to see her so happy.

"I'm not sure what there is to tell," he said, laying the hammer on top of the tiny, white dresser. "She was a good wife. I loved her."

"What happened?"

He drew in a deep breath, debating how much to say. As he exhaled, the decision was made. He'd tell her everything, and if she blamed him, hated him, it would be no more than he blamed and hated himself.

"Come and sit, okay?" He turned the new rocking chair in her direction, waiting while she settled in. Her pregnancy, which grew more pronounced every day, both fascinated and terrified him. From such a moment, he'd gained Mariah, but he'd also lost his wife.

With no other chairs in the room, he slid down against the wall, knees up, facing Kelsey who sat quietly waiting for him to begin. And so he did.

"Amanda was pregnant with Mariah," he said simply. "We were ecstatic. She took good care of herself, did all the right things. The world was perfect and nothing could go wrong."

He picked at the soft carpet, remembering. His gut ached, as it always did when he thought of that time, but in more than six years he'd never discussed any of it.

"But something happened," Kelsey said softly, encouraging him as she did his daughter whenever Mariah hit a snag in her studies. That was Kelsey. Queen of the nurturers.

"Two weeks before Mariah was due, Amanda went into seizures. Full blown eclampsia, they told me later. I found her on the bedroom floor, unconscious. No one knew for sure how long she'd been there. Maybe all day. She was barely alive."

The memory of his beautiful, young wife lying in a crumpled heap next to the bed where they'd made love still haunted him.

Kelsey reacted, leaning forward, shock and sadness on her face. "Oh, Ryan, how awful for you."

He gazed up at her blue-green eyes, saw himself reflected there in shimmering pools of sympathy. He didn't deserve sympathy or understanding. The tragedy was his fault.

"It was eight o'clock at night, Kelsey," he said, harshly. "I should have been home hours before."

He'd bent over Amanda's body, frantically calling her name. He could almost hear his own voice begging her to be all right, screaming for someone, anyone to save her. In the end, no one had.

"You weren't to blame, Ryan."

"I wish I believed that." They'd lived in a different house then. He'd sold it, furniture and all, and never went back. "The doctors took Mariah by emergency caesarian. She was tiny, pink and perfect, thank God."

The only thing that had kept him sane in the days to come was the knowledge that his child needed him.

"They did everything possible for Amanda, but I'd found her too late. She never regained consciousness."

"I'm so sorry. I don't even know what to say. Words seem impotent in the face of such a tragedy."

He looked down at his hands, studying the place where Amanda's ring had once circled his finger. "You've had your share of loss, too."

"Yes, I suppose." Her voice held a strange hesitation that he couldn't comprehend. "Like Mariah, my child will never know one of her parents. That's a sad thing."

"Your baby will be strong, too, like Mariah. Like you."

"Does she know her mother died in childbirth?"

A knot of dread tightened in Ryan's gut. "I don't know. I hope not. I'll never tell her. That's a heavy load to hang on a little kid."

"Hasn't she ever asked questions?"

"Some. I've showed her the photo albums and videos and

told her every funny story I can remember about Amanda. We wrote a journal together about her so Mariah could read it anytime she wanted."

The corner of Kelsey's lips tilted. "What a sweet thing to do."

"Yeah, that's me, Mr. Sweet."

Kelsey slipped from the chair to her knees. "Don't beat yourself up anymore, Ryan. You loved her. You did everything you could for her. And you gained an incredible daughter."

"But I wasn't home when she needed me most. She was alone and dying and I wasn't there to help her."

After he'd buried Amanda, he'd buried himself—in work and in caring for Mariah. In those days and since, work had become his solace, the only thing he was good at, the only place where he felt in control.

Not once in six years had he ever considered moving on with his own life. Not until he'd met Kelsey.

She placed a hand on his cheek. Tears glistened in her eyes. The idea that the tears were for him washed over Ryan in waves of sweetness.

"Do you think Amanda would want you to wallow in guilt for the rest of your life?" she asked softly.

A sad smile lit him from within. "She would kick my butt."

Kelsey made a sound between a sniff and a laugh. "I would have liked your Amanda."

Yes, she would have. And Amanda would have liked Kelsey, as well. She would be pleased, too, with the love Kelsey showed to their child.

"Ah, Kelsey," he murmured. "You're good for me. Come here." He pulled her around to sit beside him. She moved, awkwardly at first, to lean against his side. He draped an arm across her shoulders, letting his fingers play with her silky straight hair. "I thought you might hate me."

"For telling me about Amanda?"

"For causing her death."

"If you say that again, I may have to be the one to kick your butt."

He chuckled, a slow, sad kind of chuckle. "Amanda would like you. I like you, too."

He turned then and without hesitation gathered her as close as possible. The baby formed a natural, frustrating barrier, but Kelsey maneuvered her belly to one side and pressed her full breasts against his chest. She didn't hate him. She didn't blame him. Her gentle acceptance freed him in a way. He sat holding her for a long time and let the sadness wash out of him. Six years ago, he'd cried a river, but found no solace. Here in the half-formed nursery, in Kelsey's arms, he finally caught a glimpse of peace.

"I'm glad you told me."

"Yeah, me, too." More glad than he could ever explain.

He would always love Amanda, but maybe he was finally ready to love again.

The idea scared him. Kelsey was his nightmare in the flesh, a pregnant woman in his house. But she was also his joy. She'd made him human again. She'd given him a reason to laugh and to relax, to enjoy the fruits of his labor. A reason to come home.

There were even days when he lost the fear of becoming that poor kid from the back streets again.

"Now I understand why you're a little freaky sometimes about my pregnancy."

"Freaky? Me?"

Kelsey rolled her eyes. "Way freaky." She patted his hand. "But not necessary. What happened to Amanda isn't the norm."

The baby moved against his side and Kelsey placed a hand over the spot. He covered Kelsey's hand with his and felt the rise and fall of a new human being. He'd done this with Amanda, feeling the beauty that was Mariah long before she made her appearance. There was a person in there, a magical little girl who might have Kelsey's eyes or freckles. He smiled at the thought.

Mariah chose that moment to open the door. "What are you two doing up here so long?" She stopped dead still and then smiled. "Excuse me. I think I'll go watch TV. Pretend you never saw me. Carry on, please."

As she tip-toed out of the room, both adults burst out laughing.

"That was subtle," Ryan said.

"Not."

"She's crazy about you." He was afraid he might be, too.

"I love her. She's wonderful, Ryan, a real treasure of a child. You've done an amazing job as a single dad. When you first hired me, I didn't think so, but I was wrong. She wouldn't be who she is without you."

With his arm around her, he stroked his knuckles up and across the soft down of her cheek. Her skin was like nothing he'd ever touched, silk and satin and velvet.

"She's different since you came. She needed a woman's influence." He didn't bother to say the obvious. Mariah had always had a nanny, but she hadn't always had a young, motherly female who loved her. And he knew the truth of that. Kelsey loved his child.

A deep yearning invaded his chest just as Kelsey had invaded his life.

She was a widow, mourning her baby's father. No doubt, she still loved the man. She was also an employee. As Mariah's beloved tutor, she was far too important to alienate. He could not think of Kelsey Mason as a desirable woman.

The reasons entered his thoughts and almost as quickly dissipated like smoke on the wind.

She'd listened and understood, not hating him for Amanda's untimely death. She loved and nurtured his daughter in ways he couldn't. He owed her big time.

Though he'd sworn never to do it again, Ryan was certain he would explode if he didn't kiss her. As a thank you. That's all. Only as a thank you. One last time.

But when he gathered her close and pressed his lips to hers, a mocking voice in the back of his head called him a liar.

As her soft mouth responded to his, Ryan faced a hard truth: kissing Kelsey once would never, ever be enough.

CHAPTER THIRTEEN

KELSEY COULDN'T STOP thinking about that moment in the nursery with Ryan. She wasn't sure what would have happened if she'hadn't been pregnant, and the thought both thrilled and frightened her.

Even now, as they entered the Dallas Arboretum and Gardens together, she yearned to be in his arms again. At Ryan's suggestion, they'd left Mariah with his sister, a rare event but one that made Mariah happy. Kelsey had to admit, it pleased her, too, to be alone with Ryan for a change. Neither called the outing a date, but they were alone.

And while they chatted normally and exchanged smiles, the memory of that one special night pulsed between them.

Their kisses had begun with a sweet yearning, an exploration of sorts that lingered and tasted and questioned. The experience had been pure heaven and Kelsey had done her share of tasting and exploring, too. She was crazy, really, to think a man like Ryan who could have anyone would be attracted to a pregnant woman with nothing to offer. But he was. He must be. And the beauty of that knowledge filled her with wonder.

She'd also been frustrated by her pregnant body, but glad as well for that natural barrier. She didn't want to be a notch on

Ryan's bedpost, a nanny who succumbed to the charms of her employer, only to be cast aside at some later time.

But she couldn't believe Ryan was that kind of man. He'd been too kind, too solicitous, too concerned about her. And he was so gentle when he held her, when he touched her pregnant body, Kelsey had quite simply melted in his arms.

Maybe she was in denial.

The moment had been both magic and madness, but Kelsey could not have cared less that she was pregnant as an elephant and half-sitting, half-lying on the carpet with a most unsuitable man. The truth was that she loved Ryan Storm, whether he was the boy from the back streets or Dallas' man of the year.

His grief and guilt concerning Mariah's mother had touched her. She'd wanted to absorb his sorrow into herself and set him free. Maybe she wanted him free from the memories for selfish reasons, but Kelsey understood as well as anyone the shock of losing someone with such unexpected suddenness. The only difference was Ryan had loved Amanda with everything in him and probably still did. Kelsey was ashamed to admit she'd stopped loving Mark a long time ago.

What an ugly thing to know about herself. Poor Mark had lost his life, something she'd never, ever wanted to happen, but she'd only been able to mourn the loss of life, not the loss of a husband.

Ryan had mourned Amanda for more than six years.

"Are you sure you're up for all this walking?" Ryan asked, his hand on her elbow, as they strolled through the stunningly beautiful botanical gardens along Dallas' White Rock Lake. An oasis of color in the midst of the sprawling city, the gardens were as quiet and peaceful as the deep countryside.

Kelsey glanced at the tall, handsome man beside her. "Walking is good for me. I'm told the exercise makes delivery easier."

"Are you worried about that? The delivery, I mean?"

Kelsey caught her lower lip between her teeth, gnawed briefly and let go. "Not worried about the outcome, if that's what you mean. Baby and I will be fine, Ryan."

She knew he still compared her to Amanda.

"Even if all goes well—"

She interrupted him. "Not if, when."

He gave her a lopsided grin. "Okay, when all goes well, labor still isn't a day in the park."

"True, and I think most women are apprehensive." Sometimes she was terrified, but she couldn't tell him that, not with the fears he already carried. "Labor is the great unknown to a first-timer like me. Even though I read a lot and have watched the childbirth films, until I experience it myself, I won't really know what to expect."

"Will your father be there with you?"

"I suppose. We haven't discussed it."

"Why not?"

"He's not too crazy about becoming a grandfather." When she saw the frown on Ryan's brow, she hurried on. "But I'm sure he'll change his mind after the baby comes."

She wasn't sure of any such thing but her father wasn't heartless. He was simply busy with his own new life.

They walked along, admiring the glorious floral displays. Even in late winter, the gardens vibrated with life because of the mild Texas winters. As they passed beneath a long row of bowing trees, known as Crepe Myrtle Alley, they encountered four giant bronze toads spouting water. The unexpected sight made them both laugh. That was part of the magic of the Arboretum. Around each corner might be a stunning bronze sculpture, a whimsical fountain such as this, or even a quirky piece of art. At one point they'd discovered an enormous potted tree complete with gigantic watering can. Such pieces made the gardens a paradise of beauty and surprise.

Farther along the winding path, evergreen magnolias gave way to a sunken garden. They strolled the long center aisle lined with giant potted evergreen to enter a circular grassy courtyard. On the rise above them, steps led to a fountain area and still more greenery.

"What a lovely place," Kelsey mused.

She'd almost said, "What a lovely place for a wedding." Considering the situation between her and Ryan, she was glad she hadn't.

"Let's sit for minute." Ryan took her hand and led her to one of the many sculpted benches blending into the topiary trees. "And don't say you aren't tired."

"Actually, I was about to fall at your feet and thank you. My mind says go, go, go, but this extra weight around my middle wears me down." She placed a hand on each side of her lower back, arched and stretched. "That feels good."

"Maybe we should go home."

"Not until I see the gazebo." She pointed past the fountain. "It's reported to be so pretty." And romantic. But she didn't say that either.

She felt it though, the romance. Being with Ryan, holding hands, laughing and talking was more romantic than she thought possible.

The gazebo was, as Kelsey knew it would be, beautiful with a view of the lake in the distance and nothing but lush flowers and greenery around it. The inside was relatively large for a gazebo, but still small and intimate. Surprisingly, they were the only people there. Kelsey stood against one of the pillars, looking out at the choppy lake. The breeze, ever present in Texas, ruffled her hair and produced a shiver.

"Cold?" Ryan asked.

"Not really."

But he closed in, sliding both arms around her from behind

to warm her with his much bigger body. Kelsey soaked him in and secretly thanked the wind.

"I'll be there for you," he murmured, chin resting on top of her head.

"Where?" Her hands had found their way upward to stroke his sweater-covered forearms.

"When the baby comes."

Kelsey stilled. Over the lake two geese honked and flapped before skidding to a landing in a spray of water.

"I couldn't ask you to do that."

"Oh. Well. If you don't want me there..." Was that hurt in his voice?

"Ryan, it isn't that at all. I'm deeply moved that you would even offer, but I can't put you through the stress of labor. Not after what happened with Amanda."

She felt the rise and fall of his chest against her back and the gentle stir of his breath across her hair. "Some things never go away, Kelsey, but I don't want you to be alone. It doesn't seem right."

Not to her either. To have no one there to welcome this baby she wanted so badly seemed a sad insult to the child.

"Don't worry. I'll be okay." And this time, if her voice was the sad one, she couldn't help it.

With a tenderness that made her dream of the impossible, Ryan turned her toward him. Face sincere, he lifted her chin with his thumb and forefinger. "I'll be there, Kelsey."

The smile blooming inside her made its way to the outside. "I'd like that very much."

And when he kissed her, she wasn't surprised at all.

They stood together in that beautiful, romantic setting with the Dallas breeze playing tag in the trees and the bright promise of spring a breath away.

She clung to the moment, wondering if by some miracle, things could work out between them, if Ryan could ever close the door on his pain and embrace new love the way he embraced her today.

Her feet and back ached, but her heart was full. She almost wished they never had to leave this magical kingdom. But finally the time had come.

"Ready?" Ryan asked, though he made no move to release his hold.

"I want to say no, but my back won't let me."

He smiled. "Need a massage?"

"Now there's a tempting offer, but I don't know a good masseuse."

"I happen to know just the man."

"Man?" she asked, flirting. "Yummy. I think I like this idea better all the time. Is he tall and dark?"

"And impossibly handsome," he said and then nibbled her ear.

"I can't wait to meet him," she teased.

With a smile, he released her. "Just wait until I get you home."

Her stomach fluttered and the reaction wasn't the baby. "Careful, mister, that's sounding very suggestive."

"Too bad I can't suggest anything more than a massage." He flexed his fingers. "But I'm a man who knows how to improvise."

Playfully, she fanned her face. "Mercy. I may swoon."

"Then I will have you in my clutches."

Who would dream Ryan Storm knew how to play and flirt so incredibly well?

"Come on now. Your feet are getting puffy." Lovely that he noticed *that*. "We'll catch the tram back to the parking lot."

"Let's go by the gift shop first and get a little something for Mariah."

"Sure you're up to any more walking? You really need to get off those feet."

Kelsey made a face. "Don't coddle."

"Someone needs to." But he took her to the gift shop anyway where she chose a collectible doll and a charm bracelet for Mariah. Ryan also insisted on purchasing something educational and chose a kit for hatching butterflies.

"Perfect choice," Kelsey said. "We'll both enjoy that."

"So will I. Metamorphosis," he said. "Like Mariah's play."

"That was fun, wasn't it? Mariah was in her element that day." Kelsey picked up a flower planting guide and seed kit. "I love working with flowers." She wrinkled her nose at him. "And yes, gardening is educational."

He laughed. "Works for me. Then you and Mariah can release your butterflies into the flower garden."

"What a great idea. I love it." After a glance around to see that no one was looking, she tiptoed up to smack him on the lips. "You aren't such an ogre after all."

"Me? An ogre?" He quirked a finger and pointed it backward at himself.

"I once thought so."

"But now?"

"Mmm. You're much closer to human than I ever imagined."

Kelsey left Ryan to pay for the items while she excused herself to the ladies' room. When she returned, he waited, sack in hand, and all smiles.

Had she ever seen him smile and laugh so much as he had these last few days?

He reclaimed her hand, much to her pleasure, and led them to the parking area. Once in the car, he turned toward her in the seat. "I enjoyed today."

"No worries that the vast Storm empire has tumbled in your absence?"

"Having my Blackberry along helped." But he'd used the instrument only a few times and then briefly.

"There may be hope for you yet," she said.

Looking very much like his daughter, he said, "I bought something for you."

"Ryan!"

"It's not much. A trinket. But today was so nice, I wanted you to have a memento."

From the gift bag, he pulled a small jewelry case and snapped it open. Inside was a silver necklace she had admired. Dangling from a delicate filigree chain was a tiny sterling gazebo.

"Oh Ryan, what an incredibly sweet and thoughtful thing to do." She took the necklace from the box and reached to put it on. "I love it."

She loved him, but she couldn't say that.

"Let me."

She turned her back while he slipped the gift around her neck and fastened it. His hands dropped to her shoulders. He leaned forward and kissed her neck.

Kelsey shivered at the delicious sensation.

"Lovely," Ryan murmured.

"The necklace or the neck?" Fighting the sentimental tears that hovered at the back of her throat, she shifted in the seat to face him again.

"Both. You're a special lady, Kelsey. You've brought joy back into my house, back to me. I don't know where this thing between us is going, but I'd like to find out."

Her heart jumped. "But you don't fraternize with employees."

"Maybe I'll have to fire you."

She didn't know how to answer that. She needed her job and the last thing she ever wanted to do was leave Ryan's house.

When she didn't say anything, he stroked the back of her hand. "I'm kidding, sweetheart. You aren't going anywhere as long as I have a say."

"Meaning?"

"Mariah needs you. So do I."

"Even if it means fraternizing?"

"As long as fraternizing includes more days like today."

Kelsey's heart did a happy dance. Was he saying what she thought he was saying? "Do you always kiss the employees you fraternize with?"

"Yes."

"Ryan." She jerked away and swatted at him.

He laughed and pulled her back to him for a kiss. "If I'd known kissing employees was this much fun I might have started before you, but alas, you're the first."

"In that case, fraternize with me again."

He obliged, and just when Kelsey thought she'd melt into the car seat, Ryan's cell phone chirped. With an annoyed groan, he whipped it out of his jacket. "Ryan Storm."

As he listened, a strange and troubled expression moved over his features. He looked at her and then looked away.

"When? Where?" His voice was short, sharp. He looked at her again.

A terrible foreboding slithered up Kelsey's spine like a deadly snake. Ryan's gaze locked on hers, almost pleading, though she had no idea why. With his free hand, he reached out and took hers.

Something was wrong.

Kelsey tilted her head in question. "Mariah?"

He shook his head, still listening. Finally, he barked, "No. I'll tell her and get back to you."

Then he snapped the telephone shut and sat staring at it as if he wished he'd never owned one.

"Is something wrong?"

"I guess it depends on your interpretation."

What an odd answer. "What is it? Is Mariah okay?"

"That wasn't about Mariah. It was about you."

"Me? Did I do something wrong?" A pulse started low in her belly and hammered out a rhythm.

Ryan raked a hand through his hair in agitation. "I don't know how to tell you this." He took a breath, blew it out, took another.

"You're scaring me, Ryan."

"I'm sorry. It's good news. Really, it is."

"Then why are you so upset?"

"Even good news can be shocking. And you're pregnant."

That again.

He reached for her but seemed to change his mind. "There's only one way to say this." He swallowed. "Your husband is alive."

CHAPTER FOURTEEN

THE DRIVE HOME SEEMED endless. Kelsey sat in shocked silence against the passenger door, staring blindly out at the congested Dallas traffic. Over and over Ryan asked if she was okay, if she needed a doctor.

What she needed was Ryan's arms around her again, but she was still a married woman, not a widow, and that truth screamed across the seat between them. They'd been kissing, tentatively moving toward something much deeper than friendship and, all the while, she was a married woman. Five more minutes and she would have confessed her love to Ryan.

Thank goodness she hadn't. He didn't need that guilt added to the load he already carried.

But she loved him, not Mark. The truth shamed her, though she was innocent by ignorance.

Mark was alive. She should be rejoicing. Yet, all she felt was confused.

The mood was somber as they arrived home. Home. Ryan's home. The place she wanted to stay forever and yet that was no longer possible.

She collapsed on a chair in the living room. Ryan brought her a glass of water. "I'll make some more calls if you'd like and get the details."

"I'll do it."

"Of course." He stood stiffly, awkwardly as if they were strangers. Everything in her cried out to him, but she remained frozen in shock.

Ryan left the room but returned almost immediately, hovering over her as if she were about to fracture. She could feel his concern and didn't want that. She wanted his love, not his worry.

Finally, she roused and made the necessary telephone calls. Mark was alive but in poor condition in a Seattle hospital. The details were unclear and confusing but one thing was plain. She had promised to care of Mark in sickness and health. Now that he needed her so badly, she couldn't live with the guilt if she didn't respond. She had to return to Seattle and to her husband.

Ryan listened to Kelsey's soft voice, his heart ripping out of his chest. He'd only just found her, and now she would leave him forever.

Tears streamed down her face. Tears of shock, but surely of relief, too. Her husband was alive. It was the best possible thing that could happen for her and the baby she carried.

A pang of jealousy tore through him. He'd begun to think of that baby as his. Fool that he was.

He knelt in front of her and gently dried her tears.

If he loved her, and he did, he would help her through the shock and set her free without ever admitting the truth. That losing her would be every bit as hard as losing Amanda.

Kelsey couldn't remember how she'd managed to get through the next couple of days of telephone calls and arrangements. Ryan handled so many of the details even to the point of booking the nonstop flight to Seattle. When he'd handed her the ticket, she'd cried.

He was kindness personified, but he was no longer the man who had held and kissed her. He was her employer behaving in a formal, professional manner. The chasm between them nearly killed her. She lay in her bed that last night listening to the minutes with Ryan and Mariah ticking away.

Not once did he indicate in any way that he wanted her to stay. He'd made all the arrangements for her trip. He'd even driven her to the airport as if he couldn't wait for her to be gone. Then he'd wished her luck and walked away, his gleaming shoes echoing on the concrete.

He hadn't even asked her to call.

When she arrived in Seattle, rain was falling, a fit setting for her mood. She went first to the hotel Ryan had booked for her.

She fingered the tiny gazebo charm at her throat, remembering the sweet minutes before the fateful telephone call.

Her hand fell to her side.

Ryan had let her go so easily.

The bellman carried her bags to a lovely suite. She tipped him and waited while he set up the luggage rack, opened the drapes and adjusted the thermostat.

Then she was alone, staring out at the Space Needle and wondering what to say to her husband.

She lay down on the bed to rest awhile. Over and over, she glanced at the telephone and thought about calling Ryan. Each time, she changed her mind. Ryan admitted to being locked in the past with his dead wife, just as she was locked in the present with a now living husband. They had no future together. Wisdom dictated they make a clean break.

But still, she held out the hope that he would call. He was such a protector. Surely, he would telephone.

He didn't.

After a bit, she ordered room service, asking for soothing tea and toast. Her stomach was queasy from the bumpy plane ride.

She needed to rest, needed to eat, needed to hear from Ryan.

In truth, she was procrastinating the inevitable trip to the hospital. How would Mark look after all this time without proper medical treatment? According to the doctor she'd spoken with, he had suffered many injuries, including wounds to the head and face. He'd always been vain about his good looks. For his sake, she prayed he was still himself.

Though exhausted, both emotionally and physically, Kelsey knew she would not be able to rest until she'd seen him. Mustering more strength than she thought possible, she called a taxi cab and headed for the hospital.

As she tip-tapped down the corridors of the massive facility, she grew queasy again. Her belly cramped now and then, a sure sign of the difficult last few days.

"I'm Kelsey Mason," she explained to a white uniformed nurse. "I'm here to see my…husband."

The word tasted like ashes and sounded insincere.

"You look pale, Mrs. Mason. Are you all right?"

"Tired. I flew in from Dallas this afternoon." And arrived without my heart.

The nurse nodded knowingly. "I understand perfectly. Airports these days." She gave a shiver before going on. "Mr. Mason is down this hall on the left."

"Thank you." Before Kelsey could head that direction, the nurse rose and came around the desk. "Perhaps I should walk down there with you and make sure he's awake."

"How does he look?"

"Like a man who went without good medical care for several months, I'm afraid. Haven't you spoken to the doctors?"

"Yes, but I don't know what to expect. They said he'd had

amnesia. That's why he couldn't tell anyone who he was or where he belonged."

"Right. And he's still pretty muddy about the details." She knocked on a heavy door and then pushed it open without waiting for an answer. "Mr. Mason?"

A bandage swathed shadow moved on the narrow bed. Kelsey stepped closer.

"Mark?" she said, peering down into the man's face.

The world tilted, faded, and then came back into focus.

With a gasp, she grabbed her cramping stomach and tottered. The nurse's sturdy arms reached out and caught her before she fell.

"Mrs. Mason, what is it? Your baby?"

"That's not my husband."

And then her water broke.

Ryan stood in the darkness, one hand in his pocket, staring out at the golden moon high above Dallas. The nursery was unbearably quiet. No more giggles from next door. No more silly recipes for him to try. No joy at all in his house. Even his usually upbeat child had become a quiet, sad mouse.

An ache, bigger than the city, pulsed inside him.

For once, work provided no solace. No matter how hard he worked, he couldn't get Kelsey out of his mind.

Behind him was the nursery they had decorated together. Somehow this room was the only place he wanted to be.

He wished Kelsey could have taken all these baby things with her, but she didn't need them anymore. She didn't need him.

By now she was happily reunited with the man she loved. That's the way it was meant to be. Mark's reappearance was a miracle. Ryan knew he should be happy for Kelsey, but he was too miserable with himself.

Every time he stood in this room, he remembered the moment he'd fallen in love with her and the moment he'd vowed to be a father to her child if she'd let him.

She hadn't.

A spring rain storm had washed through Dallas earlier in the day and left the earth clean and humid-smelling. He'd always liked this time of year. Flowers popped up overnight, more reminders of Kelsey. She'd loved the arboretum. He'd loved being there with her.

"Daddy?" At the small voice, Ryan turned. Mariah, dressed in the blue nightgown Kelsey had chosen, stood silhouetted in the doorway.

"Hey, peanut." Although both he and Kelsey had tried to explain as best they could, Mariah could not accept that Kelsey would leave. Every day she expected her to return and used this untouched nursery as her proof.

She hovered in the doorway, uncertain. "Are you okay, Daddy? It's dark in here."

Not as dark as his mood. He snapped on the Mother Goose night-light.

"Are you ready for bed?" he asked. He'd done his best to keep the tradition of snuggle time.

"It's not the same without Kelsey," Mariah said, reading his mind.

"I know." He heaved a sigh. "It's okay to miss her. I do, too."

Mariah moved into the room and picked up a soft, stuffed sheep, clutching the white toy in both hands. "I've been giving the situation serious consideration, and I've come to a conclusion."

He'd known that little brain was mulling by the way she'd gone silent and sequestered herself in Kelsey's room. None of the half dozen extracurricular activities Kelsey had gotten her involved in could lure her out. Even the new nanny service held no interest.

"What conclusion would that be?" Hopefully, it meant closure for both of them. Time to move on. To get over what couldn't be.

"She's dead."

"What?" he jerked his head up so quickly his neck throbbed.

"Kelsey loved us. She wouldn't stay away unless something bad had happened." Fat tears gathered on her lower lids and shimmered there. "Her baby killed her like I killed Mommy."

Ryan's knees went weak. All the air whooshed out of him. "No, Mariah, no." He crouched in front of his now sobbing daughter and gently drew her against his chest. "You didn't kill your mommy. Where did you get such an idea?"

"It's true. I always knew I was to blame, but I didn't want to upset you by asking for details."

"Your mom was sick, Mariah. She died." If anyone was to blame, it was him, not his child. "None of that was your fault. You were the good thing she left behind."

He grasped her trembling shoulders to look into her face. All these years he'd never dreamed his baby carried such a terrible load behind the Pollyanna attitude. "I want you to understand this, Mariah, and settle the issue in your mind. You are not responsible for your mother's death. Do you understand?"

She sniffled, wagging her head from side to side. "Kelsey wouldn't leave us, Daddy. She wouldn't. I just know it. She has to be dead. She hasn't even called."

The clear confusion between Kelsey and her own mother wasn't lost on him, but he didn't know what to do. "We've talked about this before, Mariah. I know things didn't work out the way we'd hoped—"

"You loved her, too, didn't you, Daddy?"

"Yes," he admitted. "I did."

"And you wouldn't tell me if she was dead. You wouldn't want me to be upset. I know you, Daddy. You're always trying to protect me. Did you ever consider that her baby might need us?"

The words, so grown-up, but so wrong, set off another paroxysm of sobs.

Ryan gave a groan of despair. "Kelsey is okay. I promise."

"Can we call her?"

His first instinct was to say no. The reminder that she was happily married would be too much to bear. What if he cracked and blurted out the truth? They would both be so embarrassed and the truth would do no good.

"Please, Daddy. If I can talk to her, I'll know she's alive. Please let me call her. I won't even ask her to come back if you don't want me to. I'll be the best little girl in Texas."

How could he say no to that?

As uncomfortable as a conversation with Kelsey would be, he had no choice. He had booked the hotel himself. With her husband in the hospital, she was likely still staying there.

He punched in the numbers. No answer.

The failure only solidified Mariah's certainty. She slithered to the floor and sat with shoulders stooped, staring at the toy sheep. "I told you."

"We'll try later."

"It is later, Daddy. Kelsey should be in her hotel by now. Remember how her feet get puffy at night? She would be resting."

Maybe she was at the hospital with her husband. Or maybe something *had* happened.

He didn't share either thought with his daughter. Instead, he punched in the number of the hospital and asked for Mark Mason's room. He hung up more bewildered than ever.

There was no Mark Mason listed as a patient at the hospital. Ryan's head reeled with the information. This couldn't be. He'd spoken to a doctor himself.

Mariah studied his expression, her bottom lip aquiver. "It's bad news, isn't it?"

He pushed in the hotel again, this time trying the desk. To his horror, Kelsey's room was still reserved in her name but according to the clerk, she had not been there since the day she checked in.

Why would she leave and not return? Where could she be? Where was her wounded husband?

Fear swept through him as Mariah's morbid words returned. A woman could die in childbirth. He'd lived through the nightmare before. It could happen.

Dear God, don't let it happen to Kelsey.

Once again, he opened his telephone and pressed in numbers. As he listened to the connecting brrr, he stroked his daughter's hair back from her tear-stained face.

Maybe he was crazy. But Mariah would have no closure until she made connection with Kelsey. Neither would he.

No matter how difficult another meeting would be, he had to do this for his child.

"Better get some sleep, peanut. In the morning, we're going to Seattle." When hope backlit her eyes, he said, "And we're going to find Kelsey."

CHAPTER FIFTEEN

KELSEY TIPPED THE BELLMAN and on wobbly legs entered the hotel room. Taking care of business after having a baby was exhausting, especially when that business involved having your husband declared legally dead.

She'd been shocked to discover the man in the hospital was not Mark but a sailor who had accompanied him. Together with authorities she had spent the last two days trying to unravel the confusing state of events. Apparently, after the boat exploded, both men had eventually been picked up by some non-English speaking fishermen and taken to their remote island village. One of the men, now believed to be Mark, had died. The other man was in such bad condition that he had not known who or where he was for months. For reasons they might never know, the sailor carried Mark's identification.

Once again, she was filled with grief for the loss of life. Mark was gone. Regardless of how troubled their marriage, he had not been an evil man. He certainly hadn't deserved to die in such a tragic manner.

Thank goodness, the authorities had contacted her first and not Mark's brother in Nova Scotia. She didn't wish the stress of the last week on anyone. Now her brother-in-law would simply have the closure they all needed instead of living through the emotional roller coaster of believing Mark was alive, only to have him dead again.

She shuddered. The truth was too awful to take in.

The only good thing was the finality. Even the insurance company agreed that the case was resolved.

A mewing sound issued from the tiny bundle in her arms. "Shh, my precious."

With her heart full of love, she kissed the velvety forehead of her baby girl, placed her on the bed and curled up next to her.

The perfect pink angel squirmed and mewed again, tiny fists flailing as Kelsey unwrapped her. Her heart broke to know this child would grow up without even knowing her father, just as Mariah had never known her mother.

Thoughts of Mariah and Ryan were never far away, and like always, the memories flooded in. She missed them both with a gut-wrenching pain.

She thought of the nursery back in Dallas, ready and waiting for this baby. Here in Seattle, her child had so little. In time, they would be re-established, but today they were virtually homeless.

Tears gathered and ran down her cheeks. For the last few days, she'd done nothing but cry. Seattle no longer felt like home. The adage that "home is where the heart is" was true. Her heart was in a Dallas town house with a workaholic man and a genius child.

Were they okay? Had Mariah really understood why she'd had to leave? What would the new nanny-slash-tutor be like? Would Ryan fall in love with her?

The last thought stabbed her through the chest.

She thought about phoning Ryan to tell him both the good and the sad news. He'd want to know about the baby, wouldn't he? But how would he respond to the news that she was, once again, a widow?

Twice, she picked up the phone, but put it down again. He hadn't called. He hadn't left any messages. He'd shuttled her off with a one-way ticket and let her go without a backward glance. Any thoughts she'd had that he might be falling in love with her had been nothing but romantic fantasies. He'd let her go too easily. She'd been a favored employee and nothing more.

Fingers of one hand holding to the silver gazebo, Kelsey snuggled down beside her baby for a nap. Only sleep brought her peace. Her mind slowly entered the hazy haven right before total unconsciousness.

The telephone jangled. The baby jumped. Kelsey frowned. Probably more lose ends to tie up. They could wait.

The sound faded. Kelsey and baby both relaxed again until someone knocked on the door.

With a weary sigh, Kelsey swung her feet over the edge of the bed and sat, brushing her hair down with both hands.

"Who is it?"

A muffled voice replied, "Ryan and Mariah."

She whipped the door open. As soon as she knew it was really them, she burst into tears.

"Whoa. Hey. Don't." Ryan's bewilderment only made her cry harder. Kelsey covered her face with both hands. She didn't know why she was crying, but she couldn't stop. Seeing him again was rain after a long dry spell.

Grabbing her by the shoulders, Ryan backed her into the room, kicking the door shut behind them. She didn't know why they were here, but she needed them—she needed him. Without further thought, she walked into his arms and buried her face in the rough fabric of his blazer. The wonderful smell that was only Ryan wrapped around her. The strong hands that had helped her put together a nursery alternately rubbed and patted her back. He didn't speak. He simply let her cry.

Oh, and she felt so secure and comforted to dump her stress and hurt on stronger shoulders. Shoulders that she was convinced cared for her, even if he didn't love her as she loved him.

Kelsey was vaguely aware that Mariah accompanied him into the room. Her eyes had gone wide and worried when Kelsey fell apart. She had to get hold of herself before she scared them both to death. Gulping, she swallowed back a fresh round of tears.

Finally, she gathered her composure and stepped back. "I'm sorry."

He waved off the apology. "What's wrong? Why are you here?"

Knees shaky, she sat down in the nearest chair and indicated for him to sit, as well.

"I was about to ask the same of you."

"You first," he said. "We've been trying to reach you."

Hope soared. "You have?"

"Mariah is beside herself with worry."

Oh. So he was here only for Mariah. Okay. Fair enough.

"For some reason," Ryan went on, "she became convinced that you had died in childbirth."

Like her mother. Kelsey glanced at the little girl, her throat filling with compassion. Poor little lamb.

"Nothing I said could change her mind. She thought I was lying to protect her."

"Oh, Mariah." Kelsey took the child's hand and tugged, bringing her close for a hug. "I'm very well, as you can see."

As well as anyone could be with a broken heart.

Mariah had already focused in on the pink bundle sleeping on the bed. "You had the baby. Is she a girl?"

"Yes, I did. A little early, but she's fine." The baby sister you wanted. "Come and meet her."

Kelsey felt Ryan move beside her as together they stood over the new arrival.

"She's pink," Mariah said, matter-of-factly. "That's my favorite color."

Kelsey smiled. "Mine, too."

"You need to bring her home. Her nursery is lonely."

Kelsey glanced at Ryan and then away.

"Want to watch her for me while your daddy and I talk?"

"May I?" Mariah asked in wonder. When Kelsey nodded, she climbed very carefully onto the edge of the bed and sat motionless, staring down at the new baby.

"You weren't due for another three weeks," Ryan said. "Is this why we couldn't reach you? You were in the hospital."

"Partly. I'm so sorry Mariah went through that agony. What made her think such a thing?"

Ryan hung his folded hands between his knees. "Me, I guess. I've always tried to shelter her from the details, so instead of getting the facts straight, that mind of hers filled in the gaps with erroneous information. All this time, she's believed she killed her mother."

"Oh no." Kelsey spun toward Mariah. "That's not at all true, sweetie. Do you know that now?"

The child nodded, then pressed a finger to her lips. "You must talk quietly. The baby jumped."

"Okay," Kelsey whispered, amused. "Excuse us."

As she turned back to face Ryan, he asked, "How is your husband?"

Her hand flew to her lips. He didn't know. He had come all this way for Mariah's sake, and he didn't know.

"The man in the hospital wasn't Mark."

"I don't understand."

"Neither did I. In fact, the shock sent me into labor."

Ryan started to go to her, but forced himself to stay seated. He wanted so badly to hold her again, but knew better. She was the wife of another man, and he would not be a home wrecker even if she would allow it. She wouldn't, but she had been through a rough time during the last few days. No wonder she'd been shocked into labor. She'd gone to Seattle to reunite with the man she loved only to find another man in his place.

"Where is Mark, then? Why aren't you with him?"

"Because Mark died in that blast just as we always thought."

The words bounced around the room like a rubber ball on concrete. The reality seeped into him. She *was* a widow. Was it wrong to be so happy about that? Though the urge was strong to yank her against him and kiss her until she promised to go home with him, he controlled himself. She was a grieving widow. Not once but twice. No wonder she'd cried so brokenly.

He scooted the wooden chair closer to her. She might be someone else's widow, but she needed his comfort. At least, he told himself she did.

"Tell me what happened."

Kelsey launched into a tale that would make some tabloid reporter delirious with joy. In the end, he was convinced, as she was, that her husband had perished in the accident.

"I'm sorry for your loss," he said, hearing the stiffness in his voice. How was he supposed to react? To whoop with joy would be both cruel and inappropriate. "This must be doubly difficult. Losing the man you loved, not once but twice."

The last sentence cost him, but he said it anyway as a reminder that her heart belonged here in Seattle.

"I lost Mark a long time ago, Ryan." She stared off into space, thinking for a moment before going on. Her expression was heartbreakingly sad. "He didn't love me, you know."

The comment jolted him. He leaned forward. "What?"

"Our marriage was over long before he died. The pregnancy was my foolish way of trying to recapture what was lost. I only made matters worse."

He stared at her, uncomprehending. "Did you love him?"

"I'll always be sad that a man died, but I hadn't loved him for a long time."

The ramifications thundered through his veins. She didn't love her dead husband? And hadn't for a long time?

The taste of her kisses lingered in the back of his mind. She'd never kissed him like a woman in mourning. She'd kissed him like a woman in love.

Could it be possible?

Before he could examine all the details and make an informed decision, his daughter appeared between him and Kelsey.

Hands on hips, she said, "Daddy, just tell her you love her so we can all go home." She whirled toward Kelsey. "Daddy and I love you. Do you love us?"

Kelsey's startled gaze flew from Mariah to him where she locked on. "Ryan? Is this true?"

"If we've embarrassed you or spoken out of turn, please say so and we'll go quietly back to Dallas and leave you alone, but if you care for us, if there's a chance for you and me—"

"Yes," she said simply, rising from the chair to come toward him.

By the time she reached him, he was on his feet, mortification turning to wonder and joy. "You mean it? You'd risk a future with a stuffy workaholic?"

"Only if he loves me as much as I love him."

"Is more than life itself enough?"

"It'll do for starters." Then she wrapped her slender arms around him and pressed her lips to his in a kiss that answered all his questions.

For a few glorious minutes, they basked in the knowledge of love realized, but then a small cry interrupted.

With a wry grin, Kelsey pulled away. "Hold that thought while I check on Amanda. I fed her a bit ago. She's probably wet."

Ryan followed her to the bed and watched while she gathered the squirming infant into her arms. "Amanda? You named her Amanda?"

Kelsey's sweet smile bloomed. "In her memory and as a thank you."

Ryan thought he would burst with happiness. "A thank you?"

"For the gift of Mariah." She touched his daughter's hair with a kiss and received a beaming smile in return. "And for loving you so well."

"You're a special woman, Kelsey Slater."

"Want to fraternize with me?" she teased.

"As a matter of fact, I do." He kissed her upturned face. "Let's take our girls and go home."

EPILOGUE

LATE ONE EVENING, ON A DAY when butterflies kissed the camellias and cannas and the orange sun hovered over glistening White Rock Lake, Kelsey smoothed a nervous hand down the pencil skirt and waited for the music to begin. Today was her day and she felt like a princess.

She'd gotten her figure back after Amanda's birth and loved the fit of her cocktail-length dress. Shimmery blue, the gown was cut modestly low in front and back, the neckline edged with delicate beading. At her throat, she wore the silver gazebo necklace Ryan had given her. She touched it, remembering that beautiful day when they'd fallen so wonderfully in love.

And today here at the Dallas Arboretum, they would finalize the depth of that love. They would be wed. She would be joined forever with the man who filled all the empty places inside her. He claimed she did the same for him, and she felt powerful and womanly knowing it was true. Together, they were complete.

"Almost time, Kelsey." Ryan's sister Michelle grinned mischievously at her. They'd become good friends and Kelsey was thrilled to have her as maid of honor. They stood together outside the sunken garden waiting to walk down the center aisle and up the rise of stairs where the ceremony would take place.

"I hope I don't trip on the steps," she said, gnawing her lip.

"If you do, my brother will do something incredibly romantic and overprotective like rush to your side and carry you up the steps in his arms."

"Hmm. Maybe stumbling wouldn't be so bad after all."

Ryan had rented the entire area around the gazebo and had it closed off to the public because of unwanted press coverage. The two of them seemed to have generated considerable gossip, owing to Ryan's status and Kelsey's recent bizarre tragedy. She had no idea how the press learned of such things, but they always did.

The Dallas tabloids had had a field day when the news of the engagement broke. Some called it romantic. Others used terms like scandalous and tragic. The tycoon and the tutor. The widow and the wonder boy.

Ryan, who loved privacy almost as much as he loved his family, did not appreciate the attention. Kelsey laughed, reminding him that someone else would soon capture the reporters' fancy and he would be old news.

He'd replied, "As long as I'm never old news with you."

As if he could be.

The string quartet began to play.

The butterflies had left their flowers and now fluttered inside her stomach. She drew in a breath, found the air redolent with the sweet scent of camellias and pungent evergreen.

"Here we go." Michelle waved four fingers over her shoulder as she started down the grassy aisle. Guests seated on both sides turned to watch. For a man of Ryan's status, the gathering was small, but that was the way they'd both wanted it. Small and intimate, with only those present who truly cared.

Kelsey looked up to see the minister, the best man and Ryan step into sight on the platform. Her heart lifted as it always did whenever she first saw him. Tall and handsome in his tux and crisp white shirt, he was more than she'd ever dreamed of and all she ever wanted in a mate.

Mariah stood at her father's side, lovely and innocent in a long, full dress in the same shimmery blue material as Kelsey's. A blue butterfly fluttered and hovered around the little girl as if she were a desired flower. Mariah saw it and smiled.

"Ready, Dad?" Kelsey said, sliding her hand into the crook of her father's arm. Though she wondered if they'd ever be close, relations with her father and stepmother had warmed. She was certain Ryan had a part in that, and she was thankful. Her happiness couldn't be complete without her family.

She looked toward the congregation where her stepmother sat on the front row of chairs, holding Amanda. The baby lay across the woman's shoulder, blissfully unaware of the magnitude of this day. Today she would gain a loving, protective father in Ryan Storm, a man who'd loved her long before she was born.

They started forward, the strains of Pachelbel's "Canon" sighing on the sweet evening wind. As they passed her stepmother, Kelsey paused to lift Amanda into her arms. Then she locked her focus on her handsome groom, moving toward him with joy and assurance. He, too, only had eyes for her. His smile, gentle and a bit shy, called to her.

As she reached the place where he waited, he took her hand and squeezed, their secret signal of love.

But the ceremony did not begin in the usual manner. The minister said, "Ladies and gentlemen, Ryan and Kelsey had asked that we do something special during their ceremony. Today as they are joined together in holy matrimony, a family is also being created." He smiled at Mariah who shifted nervously from one foot to the other. "Ready, Mariah?"

Mariah nodded and stepped into the circle that was Ryan and

Kelsey, Mariah and Amanda. The blue butterfly followed, unbothered by the presence of humans, adding beauty to the ceremony.

Kelsey felt a swell of love so pure, tears gathered. She'd promised Ryan she wouldn't cry, but that was a promise he would have to let her break.

They joined hands, the three of them with tiny Amanda between them while the minister asked a special blessing on their union as a family.

When that was finished, Ryan slipped a delicate chain over his daughter's head. A small gold engraved ring dangled from the center. "Mariah, this necklace ring is made especially for you and another for your baby sister. Your new mother and I chose it for this occasion. Wear it always as a symbol of our new family, united today in love."

Kelsey bent to kiss her new daughter. "I love you," she whispered.

"Then stop crying," Mariah whispered back, loud enough to make the congregation titter. "I love you, too."

Ryan kissed the baby and placed her in Mariah's outstretched arms just as they'd planned. Proudly, the big sister accompanied by her new grandfather carried Amanda to a seat where they would sit until the ceremony ended. The blue butterfly remained behind almost as if it wished to add a blessing to the day.

For some reason, the lovely insect made Kelsey think of Amanda, a gentle lady whose beauty, like that of the butterfly, had only remained for a season.

The vows began then, those simple, age-old words from the Bible that join a man and woman together in holy matrimony. To Kelsey and Ryan the meaning was brand new, spoken with the sincerity that true love brings.

"I, Kelsey, take you, Ryan." Her voice cracked and she giggled with nerves.

Ryan's warm chuckle assured her he didn't mind. They grinned into each other's faces, both too happy not to show it.

When his fingers trembled during the ring exchange, Kelsey was so touched, she bent to kiss them.

The congregation emitted a sentimental *ahhh.*

Finally the last prayer was spoken and the vows completed. The wedding ceremony was over.

But as Kelsey threw herself into Ryan's open arms and kissed him with a promise for all that would come tonight and forever, the blue butterfly fluttered and quivered and settled in her hair.

And the bride knew without a doubt: the ceremony might be over.

But life had just begun.

* * * * *

*Look for more heartwarming stories from
reader favorite Linda Goodnight
in both Harlequin Romance and
Steeple Hill Love Inspired early 2009!*

Here's a sneak peek at
THE CEO'S CHRISTMAS PROPOSITION,
the first in USA TODAY *bestselling author*
Merline Lovelace's HOLIDAYS ABROAD *trilogy*
coming in November 2008.

American Devon McShay is about to get the Christmas surprise of a lifetime when she meets her new client, sexy billionaire Caleb Logan, for the very first time.

Silhouette®

Desire

Available November 2008

Her breath whistled out in a sigh of relief when he exited Customs. Devon recognized him right away from the newspaper and magazine articles her friend and partner Sabrina had looked up during her frantic prep work.

Caleb John Logan, Jr. Thirty-one. Six-two. With jet-black hair, laser-blue eyes and a linebacker's shoulders under his charcoal-gray cashmere overcoat. His jaw-dropping good looks didn't score him any points with Devon. She'd learned the hard way not to trust handsome heartbreakers like Cal Logan.

But he was a client. An important one. And she was willing to give someone who'd served a hitch in the marines before earning a B.S. from the University of Oregon, an MBA from Stanford and his first million at the ripe old age of twenty-six the benefit of the doubt.

Right up until he spotted the hot-pink pashmina, that is.

Devon knew the flash of color was more visible than the sign she held up with his name on it. So she wasn't surprised when Logan picked her out of the crowd and cut in her direction. She'd just plastered on her best businesswoman smile when he whipped an arm around her waist. The next moment she was sprawled against his cashmere-covered chest.

"Hello, brown eyes."

Swooping down, he covered her mouth with his.

Sheer astonishment kept Devon rooted to the spot for a few

seconds while her mind whirled chaotically. Her first thought was that her client had downed a few too many drinks during the long flight. Her second, that he'd mistaken the kind of escort and consulting services her company provided. Her third shoved everything else out of her head.

The man could kiss!

His mouth moved over hers with a skill that ignited sparks at a half dozen flash points throughout her body. Devon hadn't experienced that kind of spontaneous combustion in a while. A *long* while.

The sparks were still popping when she pushed off his chest, only now they fueled a flush of anger.

"Do you always greet women you don't know with a lip-lock, Mr. Logan?"

A smile crinkled the skin at the corners of his eyes. "As a matter of fact, I don't. That was from Don."

"Huh?"

"He said he owed you one from New Year's Eve two years ago and made me promise to deliver it."

She stared up at him in total incomprehension. Logan hooked a brow and attempted to prompt a nonexistent memory.

"He abandoned you at the Waldorf. Five minutes before midnight. To deliver twins."

"I don't have a clue who or what you're…"

Understanding burst like a water balloon.

"Wait a sec. Are you talking about Sabrina's old boyfriend? Your buddy, who's now an ob-gyn doc?"

It was Logan's turn to look startled. He recovered faster than Devon had, though. His smile widened into a rueful grin.

"I take it you're not Sabrina Russo."

"No, Mr. Logan, I am *not*."

* * * * *

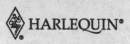

LAURA MARIE ALTOM
A Daddy for Christmas
THE STATE OF PARENTHOOD

Single mom Jesse Cummings is struggling
to run her Oklahoma ranch and raise her
two little girls after the death of her husband.
Then on Christmas Eve, a miracle strolls onto
her land in the form of tall, handsome bull
rider Gage Moore. He doesn't plan on staying,
but in the season of miracles, anything
can happen....

**_Available November
wherever books are sold._**

LOVE, HOME & HAPPINESS

www.eHarlequin.com   HAR75237

nocturne™

ESCAPE THE CHILL OF WINTER WITH TWO SPECIAL STORIES FROM BESTSELLING AUTHORS

MICHELE HAUF

AND

VIVI ANNA

———

WINTER KISSED

In "A Kiss of Frost," photographer Kate Wilson experiences the icy kisses of Jal Frosti, but soon learns that this icy god has a deadly ulterior motive. Can Kate's love melt his heart?

In "Ice Bound," Dr. Darien Calder travels to the north island of Japan, where he discovers an icy goddess who is rumored to freeze doomed travelers. Darien is determined to melt her beautiful but frosty exterior and break her of the curse she carries...before it's too late.

Available November wherever books are sold.

Silhouette®

Romantic
SUSPENSE

**Sparked by Danger,
Fueled by Passion.**

Lindsay McKenna
Susan Grant

Mission: Christmas

Celebrate the holidays with a pair
of military heroines and their daring men
in two romantic, adventurous stories
from these bestselling authors.

Featuring:

"The Christmas Wild Bunch"
by *USA TODAY* bestselling author
Lindsay McKenna

and

"Snowbound with a Prince"
by *New York Times* bestselling author
Susan Grant

Available November wherever books are sold.

REQUEST YOUR FREE BOOKS!
2 FREE NOVELS PLUS 2
FREE GIFTS!

HARLEQUIN ROMANCE®

From the Heart, For the Heart

YES! Please send me 2 FREE Harlequin Romance® novels and my 2 FREE gifts (gifts are worth about $10). After receiving them, if I don't wish to receive any more books, I can return the shipping statement marked "cancel". If I don't cancel, I will receive 4 brand-new novels every month and be billed just $3.32 per book in the U.S. or $3.80 per book in Canada, plus 25¢ shipping and handling per book and applicable taxes, if any*. That's a savings of over 15% off the cover price! I understand that accepting the 2 free books and gifts places me under no obligation to buy anything. I can always return a shipment and cancel at any time. Even if I never buy another book, the two free books and gifts are mine to keep forever.

114 HDN ERQW   314 HDN ERQ9

Name	(PLEASE PRINT)

Address	Apt. #

City	State/Prov.	Zip/Postal Code

Signature (if under 18, a parent or guardian must sign)

Mail to the **Harlequin Reader Service:**
IN U.S.A.: P.O. Box 1867, Buffalo, NY 14240-1867
IN CANADA: P.O. Box 609, Fort Erie, Ontario L2A 5X3

Not valid to current subscribers of Harlequin Romance books.

Want to try two free books from another line?
Call 1-800-873-8635 or visit www.morefreebooks.com.

* Terms and prices subject to change without notice. N.Y. residents add applicable sales tax. Canadian residents will be charged applicable provincial taxes and GST. Offer not valid in Quebec. This offer is limited to one order per household. All orders subject to approval. Credit or debit balances in a customer's account(s) may be offset by any other outstanding balance owed by or to the customer. Please allow 4 to 6 weeks for delivery. Offer available while quantities last.

Your Privacy: Harlequin Books is committed to protecting your privacy. Our Privacy Policy is available online at www.eHarlequin.com or upon request from the Reader Service. From time to time we make our lists of customers available to reputable third parties who may have a product or service of interest to you. If you would prefer we not share your name and address, please check here. ☐

HR08R

Inside ROMANCE

Stay up-to-date on all your romance reading news!

The Inside Romance newsletter is a FREE quarterly newsletter highlighting our upcoming series releases and promotions!

Click on the <u>Inside Romance</u> link on the front page of **www.eHarlequin.com** or e-mail us at insideromance@harlequin.ca to sign up to receive your FREE newsletter today!

You can also subscribe by writing us at: HARLEQUIN BOOKS Attention: Customer Service Department P.O. Box 9057, Buffalo, NY 14269-9057

Please allow 4-6 weeks for delivery of the first issue by mail.

IRNIBPA208

HARLEQUIN Romance.

Coming Next Month

**Get into the holiday spirit this month
as Harlequin Romance® brings you...**

#4057 HER MILLIONAIRE, HIS MIRACLE Myrna Mackenzie
Heart to Heart
Rich and powerful Jeremy has just discovered he's going blind, and he's
determined to keep his independence. Shy Eden has loved Jeremy from
afar for so long. Can the woman he once overlooked persuade him to
accept her help—and her love?

#4058 WEDDED IN A WHIRLWIND Liz Fielding
Miranda is on a dream tropical-island holiday when disaster strikes!
She's trapped in a dark cave and is scared for her life...but worse, she's
not alone! Miranda is trapped with macho adventurer Nick—and the real
adventure is just about to begin....

#4059 RESCUED BY THE MAGIC OF CHRISTMAS
Melissa McClone
Carly hasn't celebrated Christmas for six years—not since her fiancé
died. But this year, courageous mountain rescuer Jake is determined
she'll enjoy herself and dispel her fear of loving again with the magic of
Christmas.

#4060 BLIND DATE WITH THE BOSS Barbara Hannay
9 to 5
Sally has come to Sydney for a fresh start. And she's trying to ignore her
attraction to brooding M.D. Logan. But when he's roped into attending a
charity ball, fun-loving Sally waltzes into his life, and it will never be the
same again....

#4061 THE TYCOON'S CHRISTMAS PROPOSAL Jackie Braun
With the dreaded holidays approaching, the last thing widowed
businessman Dawson needs is a personal shopper who wants to get
personal. But Eve is intent on getting him into the Christmas spirit, and
she's hoping he'll give her the best Christmas present of all—a proposal!

#4062 CHRISTMAS WISHES, MISTLETOE KISSES Fiona Harper
After leaving her cheating husband, Louise is determined to make this
Christmas perfect for her and her young son. But it's not until she meets
gorgeous architect Ben that her Christmas really begins to sparkle....

HRCNM1008